RUDE AWAKENING

Somebody wouldn't stop ringing the doorbell. I have the loudest doorbell in the world anyway. It came with the house, and I think it was used in a Hungarian brain laundry before it was brought over here. I keep meaning to take the damned thing out, but I never get around to it. This time it just kept on ringing until I woke up. Four thirty. Since it was daylight that made it afternoon.

I got on a robe and made it to the door. My door's got dingy curtains and glass with some kind of grillwork over it, and at night you can see out without anybody seeing in if the hall light's not on. But in daytime they can see you too, and they did. There were two of them, both in dark suits, both tall, but one was blond and the other dark. They had the same look that the security officers at Boeing had: like they knew all about you and where you hid the body. Well, in my case, left it . . .

JERRY POURNELLE

RED HEROIN

C

CHARTER BOOKS, NEW YORK

1

I WAS SITTING in the office I keep in my house, drinking beer and trying to come up with a clever idea for a drainage system that wouldn't cost my client too much money, when Danny Ackerman came in. I hadn't seen him for a month, but we'd been pretty good friends, had played poker and gotten drunk together, and he'd stuck around when I had the trouble a few months before, so I was glad to see him. He's a short guy and he doesn't look like much, but people tell me he's tough. Last time I had seen him he was running a hole-in-the-wall private detective office doing mostly industrial surveillance and such while he kept trying to get a master's degree in sociology and penology at the University of Washington.

"Hi, Paul," he shouted down the hall. "Got anything to drink?"

"Sure. Come on in. I'm not getting anywhere sitting here."

My office is the living room of this old house I have in the University District. You get to it by going past the stairs in the entrance and around through the kitchen, because I keep the big sliding doors from the hall to the living room closed. The house is full of sliding doors, and built-in cupboards, and fireplaces, and wooden panels. I said it was an old house. Danny got past Tiger, a big tomcat who moved in with me one day and won't leave, and came through what used to be the dining room, to the office. He'd been there before, so I let him get his own drink, which turned out to be a glass of beer from the cooler thing some client sold me. I'll admit I've probably saved the price of the thing by buying beer by the keg, but I still say I wouldn't if the damn thing didn't make it so easy to drink beer that everyone did. He got his and sat down.

"What're you doing tonight?"

"Thought I'd scout around the District and check out the new chicks. Particularly the freshmen." Actually it's unlikely that I'd do that, though I have been known to. But Danny's the kind of guy who'd expect that answer.

"Good. Come out and play cops and robbers with me." He took a long drink.

"What? Go sit in your car and watch to see if some slob is carrying an airplane under his coat or something? No!"

"No, I mean be a real cop for the evening. I'll get you a badge and everything. You can keep it; might do you some good if they ever try to lay a ticket on you."

"Danny, you got to be crazy. How are you handing out badges?"

"I'm the new chief of police in Lathrop. Don't I look like one?"

"You look more like a crook." I said that, but I didn't mean it. One of the reasons I like Danny is that he's really a pretty good guy. I may run around with some real losers once in a while, but when you come right down to it, I don't think much of people who are just out for what they can get. That's a hell of a thing for me to say since I guess that's what I am, but at least my racket's honest. It says so in the law books.

"Here. Look." He took out his wallet, and there was a badge. Bright, shiny, with the state seal on it and everything. It had a big number "one" and said "Marshal." I looked at it, and the card in the wallet with it, which told me that Mayor E. Sundesvall had appointed Daniel J. Ackerman his true and lawful marshal and chief of police for the town of Lathrop. Danny grinned. "Told you," he said. "This thing's for real."

"Chief of how many police?"

"You would ask. Well, there's two part-time old geezers for the daytime who watch the school crossing, and there's you."

"There's me? Like hell. You live out there now?"

"Weekends. Going out tonight, but I'll be coming back in tomorrow. Come on out and ride with me, Paul. I could use some company."

"And do what?"

"Stop a fight or two, give out some tickets to speeders, put up a drunk in the tank, and have some fun. Nothing, really. Come on."

"You mean it about the badge? I've always wanted a badge."

"Yeah. Got it fixed with the mayor. You'll have to stop by with me to see him, but it's all set. Doesn't pay anything, of course."

"Of course. What time, Danny? Leaving and coming back?"

He looked at his watch. "Well, it's four now. Ought to get out there by seven and it's an hour or so's drive. I'll catch some supper and make some calls, and pick you up at six. This is Friday so the bars close at two a.m., should be quiet in an hour after that; stop at the 'Hasty' for something to eat when we get back. I'll have you home by five a.m. tomorrow. I never heard of you going to bed alone before then on Fridays anyway."

"The hell you say. I sure wish I had the life you guys dream up for me. Okay, I'll go. Provided you get me that badge. Want to eat here?"

"Thanks, no. I've got some things to do." He started out. When he got to the kitchen door, he turned back. "Got a gun? Now, there's a question for you," he added, looking at the rifle rack on the wall. "I seem to remember you have one you can carry without wheels and a tripod somewhere. Wear one, it's legal. You won't need it, but it adds to the fun." He left.

I straightened up my papers and got the drawing board cleaned off, finished my beer, and went out to eat. I like to cook, but not for just myself, and lately there'd been nobody else to cook for—or to cook for me either, for that matter. Walking down to the District, I thought about Danny's idea of fun and wondered why I had agreed to go. Well, I never had much experience with police one way or the other, and it might be a kick to be one for an evening. Anyway, Danny was fun to talk to, and he was one of the guys who had helped me out when things were rough. Why not?

The University District of Seattle has changed a lot in the last few years. When I first came here as a student it was just a district near the university, with any place that had any particular character being concentrated in a fringe a mile away, where the taverns are legal. Then it had been kind of nice for a while, with coffeehouses and folksingers' places going up. Now it was getting a sick look to it, with too many students looking sloppy like they planned it that way, and not because they didn't have enough money not to. Lately I've begun to think the studied sloppy ones outnumber the others, but they don't really. They just take up so much of the view. The war siphons off some of the good ones too, leaving a lot who got out of going over to get in everybody's way.

I ate in Eileen's. That's not what they call it now, but the name has changed so often, I can't keep track of it. It's a reasonably nice restaurant, but everybody who owns it goes broke. They're always sure they've got a gold mine, too. It ought to be one, a block from the campus, but that's the trouble. The main customers are students, and they can't afford to eat in a nice place, but they like to go to them. And take up space while they drink coffee. If you throw them out, the faculty and people who can afford to eat in a nice place won't eat there either. So, at mealtimes it's jammed, but most of the people in it don't buy anything, or just buy coffee, and sit and talk to their friends. It was early enough so it wasn't jammed.

Over in the corner there was a booth full of ex-friends of mine. They didn't know they were ex's, because it's not too good an idea to let that kind know you don't like them. They were all about my age, thirty or so, and some had been students with me. That actually put most of them a year or two older than my 28, but since my folks let the school jump me past the third grade, I've become used to being around people a year older than me.

Some of them waved and I waved back, but their booth was full so I had a good reason to sit alone. They don't usually come to Eileen's, which was one reason why I still do. I watched them while the girl went after my order.

They were all listening to a joker in a clean shirt, which set him apart from the rest right there. I thought maybe I'd known him, but I couldn't place him. Looking at them, it came to me that I had once spent a lot of time with that crowd, had even liked a few. That was back in my student days, when finding a good party where you didn't have to spend much money was important. But I managed to obtain my degree—which wasn't that easy since I really shouldn't have skipped the third grade—and go out and make a living of sorts, while these still hung around the college. One or two might still be students, or claim to be. The rest worked in bookstores and lived off unemployment, or younger girls, or whatever else they could find, and ran around supporting one obscure cause after another. They all had a cause or two, but they changed so fast I stopped keeping up with what it was the United States was doing that had to be stopped. Even when I had known them I hadn't agreed with them, of course, but I prided myself on my ability to accept anything and anybody, and so did they, so we got along. They thought it was amusing to have an ex-officer for an occasional friend. And my wife—ex-wife legally for two months, actually for three years—had got along with them fine. She loved obscure causes.

But lately, like the District, their mood had turned ugly. More and more of them seemed actually embarrassed to know me, and the last time I went to a party where many of them were, I almost got in a fist fight. So I stopped going to their parties and started eating at Eileen's instead of somewhere one of the intense ones might turn up. As I said, these were people you didn't want mad at you. Mostly they were harmless, but when they got that intense look on their faces and started talking about how the U.S. was murdering people in Southeast Asia, it made me wonder whether they'd stay harmless. I didn't want the fire department to be the way I found out.

They were pretty excited about the newcomer, so I looked at him again, and then I remembered. John Franklin Murray. Ex-paratrooper. Socialist when he was in college. Must be thirty-two, thirty-three now. Rich parents. Thrown out of Reed College when he couldn't pay the tuition, having got his folks so sick of his lectures on how they ground the faces of the poor that they cut him off. Came to the University of Washington to finish up. Last I saw of him he had gone off to work for a real far-out newspaper, something like *People's Daily*, which I understood took the Chinese Communist party line. He hadn't been a particular friend of mine, and as I remembered it, the last time he was in town he and I had had a drunken shouting match we thought was a debate. He was another good one to stay clear of. I ate and left the place, but not before one of the girls left the group and came out with me.

She was one of the younger ones, and I thought there might be some hope for her. She was about twenty, and at least she was clean, even if she did wear the black stockings and shorts with a man's shirt that makes up the uniform around Seattle for that set. She also had the long black hair and no makeup, but she was sort of pretty for all that, and having seen her in a sweater I knew she wasn't as shapeless as the outfit made her look.

"Hi, Paul. Where you been?"

"Haven't been around much, Carole. Busy making money so I can pay taxes to support your friends' unemployment checks."

"Somebody's got to. Did you know John Murray?"

"Not very well," I told her. It was after five, and I wanted to get home so I stepped out fast, but Carole kept right up with me. I liked that, because there aren't many girls who can keep up when I walk fast, and I like to walk fast. That's one of the ten thousand things that infuriated my ex-wife. "He was in school when I was, so

I met him, but I didn't know him very well. He wouldn't have thought much of me anyway. He was a real true believer even back in college.''

"He still is. That's one reason why I left. I don't think things can be quite as bad as he says. Why, he told me the FBI was watching him, that they were probably taking pictures of everybody he talked to right then."

"That's not very original, Carole. Ivar was saying that ten years ago. Come to think of it, so was John Murray. Should they be?"

"How would I know? They do bug us once in a while. Or the cops do anyway. But I don't see how we're really all that important."

"I was about to say that myself. I heard a lot of wild talk when I used to hang around with that crowd, but that's all it was. Worst thing I ever heard of them doing was stealing an outboard motor, and then they were afraid to sell it. Probably more went on that I didn't hear about, though, since everybody knows I'm square. I'm surprised you talk to me."

"Come off it, Paul. There's nothing wrong with what we're doing. This is a free country. We've got a right to protest. Maybe we even have a duty."

"Sure, Carole. And marijuana's harmless, and Bennies won't hurt you, and drinking and talking all night is more important than studying, and to hell with it. I thought so too when I was your age and nothing could cure me of it, so let's not get in an argument about it." I walked on, figuring she'd go off somewhere else. Another time I might have tried to talk her into doing something normal for an evening, but I had this bit with Danny Ackerman to get through. She kept right up.

"Really now, Paul. You used to be friends with the crowd. You still have some good friends there. I met you at one of the parties. So what's all this about how you don't like us?"

"I didn't say I don't like you," I said idiotically. "I said I didn't want to argue with you about your habits and causes. If you have to get a statement from me, I'd say you were wasting a lot of time you'll regret later; and maybe there's more to what your friends call

bourgeois morality than you think, but I am not going
to argue with you about it, and I have to get home."

"Be at the party tonight?"

"No. I have to go up north with a friend. Bye." I
really put on the steam and left her behind. Short of
running, she couldn't keep up, and although it looked
like she was going to try it for a second, she didn't. I
went on home and changed clothes.

Take a gun, Danny said, so I looked over the collection. It wasn't much of a collection, being mostly hunting rifles. I only had three handguns. I had a visitor
from the East Coast once who thought I was trying to
start a war, what with four long guns and three pistols,
but it isn't too unusual in the West. You can be in elk
country an hour's drive out of Seattle, and the hunting
is different on each side of the Cascades. On the sea-
ward side you mostly get thick brush, and you want a
heavy slow bullet. In eastern Washington there's more
flat open country, and a flat-trajectory, high-velocity
light bullet is better for the longer shots. That makes for
two rifles, and if you hunt varmints there's another.
Add a shotgun and you have four. The pistols are a little
different, but again they're usual here. The laws are different too. You don't need a permit to carry a pistol if it
isn't concealed, and there are still a few places where
nobody thinks twice if they see a holstered pistol.
Shakes up the Easterners, though. The only trouble
was, not one of the things was suitable for carrying as a
policeman. Even as a one-night, imitation, deputy policeman. There was the old .22 Colt Woodsman I had
learned to shoot with, which was out on the grounds
that a .22 is only just better than useless, except for tin
cans and maybe birds. There was a .455 Webley I got
from a mail-order house because it was cheap, and I
wanted a big caliber gun. I sometimes carried it in the
woods, heavy as it was, because we do have bear where I
go fishing and although they're more afraid of you than
you are of them, they're still big, and once in a great
while somebody gets mauled.

Finally, there was a very good 9 mm. Luger I bought

from a hungry roommate after he had a particularly disastrous night at poker. He offered it cheap, and it was a beautiful prewar piece. I've been told it's worth a couple of hundred dollars as a collector's item now, but I've never needed to cash in on it. Lugers are beautiful weapons. But they're automatics, which means you can't carry them cocked and they take both hands to get set for shooting. Automatics put out a high volume of fire which is what the military is interested in, but a policeman is usually concerned about getting off one reliable shot in five years. As a military weapon Lugers weren't so hot either. That big outside knee gets dirty if you aren't careful. The only reason the Germans adopted them was that the 7 mm. Luger, which is a police caliber, has all the same parts as the 9 mm. except for the barrel. Change that and your police weapon is a military pistol. The treaty that ended World War One forbade the Germans to have military pistols, so they used the Luger for the police and when they decided to convert, presto, a lot of 7 mm. barrels hit the ashcan. Also, the Luger can have a stock and a drum fitted to make it a very high-fire volume weapon, if you want to do it. I guess if you have a treaty looking over your shoulder you'll try anything. But it still isn't all that much gun.

Still, it was the Luger or nothing, because the chances of concealing that Webley were nil, and I didn't have a very good holster for it anyway. I took the Luger out and checked the magazine. The gun fit my hand perfectly, and I knew why I had bought it. Impractical or not, there's a deadly quality about the thing that's lacking in other handguns. And it is at least as accurate as I am, which isn't very. I also took out some cartridges and thought about whether or not to take them. Which was silly, because the chance that the gun would be anything but in the way was so small as to be zero. But, I thought, what the hell, if I'm going to be a fool I might as well be a complete one, so I found a plastic box from my fishing tackle and got eight cartridges in it, and dropped the whole mess in my pocket. Then I strapped the Luger on my left side, up high against my hip where it would be easy to carry, and buttoned down the flap of the holster. The thing was only a little easier to get at than if I had put it in the desk drawer, but at least my coat would cover it. I also put on a tie and got out a good sports coat, and there I was. It was about a quarter to six, so I sat down with a beer. Danny came right on time—just as I was finishing.

2

WE GOT INTO Danny's Rambler and pulled out. It was quite a car. He had it fitted out with a radio and a red flashing light that sat magnetically on the dashboard, and he said there was a siren. The light was removable because the insurance costs less that way. He didn't explain why. We drove out Highway 99, and the traffic was heavy so we didn't talk much. Then we went past the cemetery, and there was the neon sign "BABY-LAND," and I thought about my three-month-old kid in there and how maybe if he had lived things would have been different, and I didn't feel much like talking. I also wondered if I wanted things different, but I decided I did.

The traffic thinned out. Danny got a cigarette going, and I lit my pipe and said, "Do you know Carole Halleck?"

"Little. She's Jim Randall's girl. Or he says she is. Says he's teaching her real good, but she wasn't much when he met her. Made out she was a virgin."

"She stays around Randall and he lets her, but Danny, you know Randall has been telling us for eight or nine years now he's teaching some girl fantastic bed techniques. To hear him, he's educated every girl in Seattle."

"Maybe he has. They like him enough. Yeah, I remember Carole. She was with him at the last poker game Randall showed up at. Seemed a little nice for that crowd. I kept thinking somebody ought to get her away from them. Maybe I'll try it one of these days. Junior in sociology. I see her in class once in a while, had coffee with her in Commons the other day. Too bright for that group, but too involved with ending the war for me."

I took a long pull on my pipe. "Funny thing, Dan.

She followed me out of Eileen's tonight. John Murray's back and they were all talking to him, and when I left, she did. Couldn't shake her for a couple of blocks, but she didn't have anything to say. Hell, I hardly know her. Wonder what she wanted?"

Danny cut around a truck, dropped into second and screamed up a hill, and got back in the left lane. "Heh. Wish I had your problem. Look her up and find out. Randall can't have ruined her much. I always did want to know if he really did teach them anything; you tell me."

We laughed, and drove on. Lathrop is off the main highway on the old highway, inland about five miles from a dinky little port that used to be part of an army training camp. The only excuse for Lathrop's existence is dairies. There are a lot of them there. One of these days the new freeway will be finished and they'll start putting in houses, but we're slow about these things in Seattle. Which is nice. We swung off the highway and onto a side road, and then onto the old highway. Just after we got on it a kid in a year-old Ford screamed past us. Danny grinned.

"Three miles to my jurisdiction. Let's follow him, I bet he won't slow up when he gets to the city." He pushed the Rambler up to sixty and then eased faster to be closer. "Plug that red light in, but don't hit the switch until I tell you."

I found the wire and saw it fitted the cigarette lighter outlet. Then I saw there were three outlets on a little plate below the one that came with the car. Next to it was a switch marked "Siren." We were just entering Lathrop then. The kid didn't slow down, and I asked Danny if I should hit the light.

"No. Wait until he's downtown. Might as well let the folks see they have a marshal. I'll pull him over just past the main strip."

Up ahead I could see a few houses, then we got into a three-block long store and bar area. I thought I saw about seven taverns in the three blocks, which looked like a lot of taverns for the distance. Then Danny told me to hit it, and I turned on the switch and the siren.

The light flashed, and the kid started pulling over right then.

Danny went to the driver's side and I went around to the other in the best TV professional manner. The kid was obviously scared, and it was pretty plain why when Danny checked the registration. It was in his mother's name, and he didn't have much of a story about where he was going. Danny talked to him while I went back for the ticket book, which I handed over. Danny kept on talking.

"Yeah, sure," he was telling him. "Sure I believe your mother let you take the car. Now I'll tell you what's going to happen to you." The kid looked more scared than ever as Danny opened the ticket book. That blue uniform—I forgot to mention Danny had on an old Seattle police uniform he had worn when he was a police reservist, but with the Seattle patches taken off and his Chief badge on his breast. With the gun and handcuffs and nightstick, and a cartridge pouch on his belt, he looked pretty tough. Anyway the uniform and ticket book had the kid scared.

"Here it is," Danny told him. "Get back in that car and go home. Now. And if you're seen out again tonight you'll go to jail for the rest of it. Get."

The kid looked at him, then said "Thanks" about eight times, and got in his car. When nobody stopped him, he made a U-turn and drove slowly off. Danny laughed.

"That'll cost Lathrop a fine it could have got," he said, still laughing. We got back in his car. "But the kid'll go home too, and I don't think he'll take the car without his mother knowing it for a while. No point in giving him a ticket."

I might have said something about being softhearted, but I knew Danny hated even to be kidded about that. He was a soft touch, but he wanted people to think he was a ruthless bastard. I knew better. Once he staked a rather dumb girl, who had managed to get to be the next thing to a prostitute, to enough money to get her back to her hometown before she really got into trouble. He wanted anybody who knew about it to think he took it out in trade, but he didn't. Soft touch or not, though, he was also capable of making an arrest in the toughest bar in Seattle. He'd done that, too.

After we saw the kid off, we went to the house of the Honorable E. Sundesvall, mayor of the thriving city of Lathrop (Pop. 1032). His Honor was watching a crime show on TV, his shoes off and his feet propped up on a cheap coffee table. A dairy farmer, of course. Only kind who could be elected mayor of Lathrop. Dan Ackerman had already filled out a card saying I was a deputy marshal, and after a few pleasant words and a refused offer of beer, His Honor signed it. After we got outside, Danny turned to me and said, "Raise your right hand." I did. "Do you solemnly swear?" he asked.

"Quite often."

"Congratulations." We got in the car.

So now I was a duly authorized officer of the law, at least inside the town of Lathrop. But the badge was genuine, even if I had to shell out two bucks fifty to pay Dan for the cost of it, and who knows, I figured, I'll put it in my wallet with my driver's license. Maybe next time I'm stopped for speeding they'll see it and let me off.

We rode around a while, gave out four or five tickets to people who didn't slow down at the town limits, and then parked and walked through the main district. We stopped in every tavern. In each place, the bartender had something clever to say about baseball or the weather or something, and in between taverns we rattled doors to see they were locked. Just like the Western movies. I got the sights of the town pointed out to me, and a couple of times we talked drunks into driving slow when they went home, and it was dull as hell. Then we stopped at the police station, which was also the town hall, and I got to see the damndest thing ever: the jail. It was a cage about eight feet square, with an iron bunk in it and nothing else. It looked just like it was off a Western set. Dan explained that the town bought it from another town that had had it since before the turn of the century and finally got around to modernizing. God knows what Lathrop had before it got that thing. Anybody detained for more than overnight was taken to the county jail in Seattle, so it really wasn't as bad as it looked. I guess. But I sure as hell would hate to be locked up there.

Finally it came two o'clock and we closed up the taverns, or rather rattled the doors after the barkeeps had closed them up, and that was it. My fling as a policeman was about over. Exciting.

It was nearly three when we drove off. Nobody saw us come into town, nobody saw us leave. I remarked on that, and was told that nothing ever really happened there anyway. But it was a living, and Dan figured it might look good on his record to have been a chief of police if he ever got his degree. He figured to be a real chief of police in some small town somewhere—small, but bigger than Lathrop. Or maybe work up to being a prison warden.

"How you making out?" he asked me.

"Fine. I get enough work. More than most consulting engineers get for the first few years. And I get a little money from some patents, and now Lois and I have split up, what's there to spend money on? Got a fat fee last week for a bridge I designed for a logging road, got another one coming for some drainage suggestions for the same outfit's land. Then there's . . ." I never got to finish. The radio made some noises I didn't hear, Dan reached over and started the siren and light, and off we went. That radio had been going all night, but he had it turned so low I couldn't hear anything. A couple of times he had called the county dispatcher to let him know where he was, and when he did I listened close and could just make out what came in, but I wasn't used to the thing.

"What in hell you doing?" I asked. I thought it was a pretty reasonable question, because we were screaming down the highway at eighty or more.

"Didn't you hear that? Officer needs assistance down at Richmond Landing. That's only a couple or three miles from here."

Richmond Landing is that crummy little boat harbor west of Lathrop. I had put in there a couple of times when it was just rotten piers, before somebody bought it and started renting out berths to people living on the coast around there. Some developments had gone in in that general area, and maybe the guy was making money, but there sure wasn't anything at the Landing I could think of. Just a shack of a general store and the docks. I couldn't even remember any particularly good boats there.

By the time I'd remembered everything about the place, we were coming up on it. Ackerman could sure drive, I'll say that for him. The headlights picked up a sheriff's deputy car with the doors open. Then we saw a uniformed deputy lying in the road, one arm still inside the cruiser. Right after that there was a flash off to the right, and another just ahead of us. The flat crack of pistol shots came with them.

"What the hell?" I yelled.

Dan whipped the car off to the left side of the road, popped open his door, and was out on the ground a second later. I wasn't behind him by much. Policeman I never had been before, but I was glad to see that what I learned in the army was still with me: Hit the dirt when there's shooting.

I got out the Luger while we took stock of the situation. The big knee made a satisfactory click when I cocked the piece, but I still hadn't the foggiest what to do with it. Then we heard a yell from whoever was off to the right."

"Peterson, sheriff's office, here. They're in right ahead of you. Watch them, they got my partner." The deputy's voice had a strain in it. He's been hit, I thought.

Dan waved me off to the left. He was impatient as hell, and I didn't have time to tell him I didn't want in on this. "Ackerman, Lathrop police here. Heard your call. We'll move in on them." Dan got up to a crouch and started down the shallow ditch by the left side of the road. There was another flash from the deeper ditch on the right side just ahead of us, then another from somewhere behind that, so I knew there were two of them.

It wasn't my night, but hell, you can't run out on

friends. I like to tell people stories about when I was in Vietnam, but I usually neglect to mention that I was an advisor on construction and never saw a Cong to know one. They took a few shots at me, but from a long way off and the only times I ever shot back I was sure I hadn't hit anything. So this was my first real combat as opposed to training exercises, but it was a little like a drill. When Dan threw himself flat and started shooting toward the gun flashes, I moved parallel to the road and on ahead of him till I was past them. When I got in position, I took a shot myself, and Dan lit out across the road after them. He got to the ditch and somebody stood up. Danny shot him and went past, and there were two shots from the bushes and Danny was down, and the guy who called himself Peterson was in the road shooting. There was another shot from the bush, and I emptied the Luger into the spot where the light came from. Feeling stupid for firing myself dry, I got the magazine out of the Luger and started to push cartridges into it. I had the thing half-loaded when I realized it was awful quiet.

I finished loading and slapped the magazine into the Luger. The weapon's designed for quick reloads. When it's emptied the knee stays up until you put a magazine with shells in, after which you can push it home and she's ready to fire again. Waving the thing in front of me, I looked around the road. Nothing moved. Dan was sprawled in the ditch, and the deputy was right in the middle of the road, and both were still as hell. The guy Danny had shot was also in the ditch, almost touching Dan's feet, and I couldn't hear a thing from the bushes.

This was a hell of a situation. I figured I ought to wait until somebody else responded to the radio call, but that could take ten or fifteen more minutes. The whole firefight hadn't lasted two or three. In fifteen minutes Dan might be dead, if he wasn't already. So I did the bravest thing I've ever done. I stepped out of my cover and ran across the road, plunged past it, and charged up behind the bush where all the shooting had come from.

There were two people there, and they weren't moving. I didn't know if I had hit both of them or just one, but it seemed safe to make a light, and I turned on the big flashlight. They had on faded denims and sport shirts, and one had a poplin jacket on, and they still didn't move. I went out to see Danny, but I didn't bother to stop. He had a hole where his left eye had been and it wasn't pretty at all. I went past him to Peterson.

Deputy Peterson was still breathing, but it didn't look good. He had a big stain all over the lower part of his shirt, and I think he must have been hit before Dan and I arrived. How in hell he called to us and got up is beyond me, but I once saw a Vietnamese villager walk in from two miles out with two bullet holes in his chest, so I guess it can be done. While I was trying to figure out something to do, he gave a kind of jerk and every muscle in his body contracted at once, and he was dead too. That bastard in the bushes must have been some shot, I thought. I was sort of glad I had emptied the gun at him. Then I went off in the bushes myself and got rid of all my dinner and everything else and wished I had eaten more because it wouldn't stop and wouldn't stop.

I don't know how long that kept up. There was still nobody around, but I thought I could hear sirens off in the distance. I went back to Dan, but I didn't look at him. The punk lying near him stirred a little, and I thought, well, at least there's one survivor. He was too close to Danny though, so I went back to the other two and looked around. Neither one of them was moving. Then I noticed a little leather bag, like the ones doctors carry. I guess I thought it might be a doctor's kit and maybe I could do something with it. Anyway I opened it. It was full of little packages in waxed paper, and when I opened one of them it spilled out a white crystalline powder. I've never seen the stuff before, but I've heard it described often enough. Heroin. The bag weighed over five pounds. That made it over two kilos of heroin. I was holding about a hundred thousand dollars.

I could begin to see why these guys had started shooting, even if I wasn't sure what the sheriff's boys were doing down here. Boys. Then I remembered there had been two deputies, and I ran back to the police car, still carrying the bag. By now I could hear sirens back down the road, and I was pretty sure it wouldn't be long before I had help. I put the bag in the deputies' car and started to look at the other cop. It was hard to see what was wrong with him. He seemed to be breathing all right. I looked at him carefully and saw a neat little hole in his midsection, but there wasn't much blood. I didn't figure I could do anything for him. With gut shots there isn't much an untrained man can do anyway, or so they told me in the first aid courses we had to take in the army. The sirens were getting louder, and somebody who knew what he was doing would be there pretty quick.

The whole thing was getting to me. From where I stood I could see three dead bodies, a wounded cop, and a bag of heroin. My little tin badge was perfectly legal, provided I could get somebody to listen to me tell about it, but it was a pretty thin story. On top of it all, I was starting to get sick again, and the last thing I wanted to do was talk to the police, and probably spend all night telling them about something I didn't know one damn thing about: Danny was dead, and I'd just killed a man I never saw before. All in all it was too much for me.

What I'm trying to do is explain something I can't explain to myself. Call it shock, call it being in a daze, but I wasn't, or just say I was sick of the whole scene, but having done the bravest thing I'd ever done, I proceeded to do the stupidest. Leaving the bag in the deputies' car, I walked into the bushes, found out I wasn't quite going to be sick, and instead of coming back out on the road, I started away from there just as I saw headlights and a flashing emergency light round the curve up the road. As the car stopped next to the deputies' cruiser, I took off away from the whole scene.

3

I DIDN'T GET far before I wanted to go back, but then it hit me just how dumb this all was. Here I was, wandering around with a just-fired Luger under my coat, and right behind me were two dead cops and another unconscious. I could be dead before I ever got to a station house, or even managed to start an explanation, if the wrong types had arrived on the scene. Sure, most police are not like that. Sure, I had a good story, if you pass my running off instead of waiting for the police. But I had exactly one life and there are cops who won't listen when they think they've found a cop killer. There are a lot of country boys in uniform in some of our farm areas, and looking at that battlefield would make anybody edgy. I wouldn't blame them. I figured I had better get the hell out of there and explain over a telephone.

That left me with a problem. It was twenty miles easily to my house, and it was after three in the morning. Figuring four miles an hour if I could keep it up, and that's a fast pace, it would be after eight before I could get there, and they might be looking all over for me. Or for somebody, and I was a pretty suspicious character out there that time of night.

From what I remembered of the countryside, there should have been a railroad running along the edge of Puget Sound, and that couldn't be more than a couple of hundred yards from me. I cut off in that general direction, through scrub and weeds, and pretty soon I saw the water about forty feet below me. It didn't take long to get down the bluff, there were trails every so often, and then I started along the tracks. It wasn't much of a plan, but it was all the plan I had.

I walked till it was daylight. I won't say it didn't take

something out of me, but I still fish and hunt a bit, and a civil engineer doesn't spend all his time at a desk, so it didn't kill me. When it got light, I cut back toward the highway and found out I was inside the limits of the bus system. Nothing seemed to be happening, and even on Saturday there are people who take busses. I stayed off the highway, walking along residential streets like I lived around there, and when it got to be 8:30 I caught a bus and went home.

Once there, I was so damn tired I just didn't want to face a lot of questions. Nobody seemed to be looking for me, so I took a shower and went to bed. As I lay down, it came to me there was no reason for anybody to look for me anyway. I didn't figure the honorable mayor would remember my name, and even if he did, I could be surprised as hell and say I left Danny in my own car right after two o'clock. That way I didn't become involved, and that would be best. A consulting engineer needs his name in the papers in connection with dope smuggling like a Communist needs to be given a patriotism medal by the DAR. Nobody would understand. If I'd stayed there, I could have been a hero, but there isn't much heroism in running out. The hell with it. I remembered to stuff the Luger into a place I didn't think anybody would find it, and then I went to sleep.

Somebody wouldn't stop ringing the doorbell. I have the loudest doorbell in the world anyway. It came with the house, and I think it was used in a Hungarian brain laundry before it was brought over here. I keep meaning to take the damned thing out, but I never get around to it. This time it just kept on ringing until I woke up. Four thirty. Since it was daylight that made it afternoon.

I got on a robe and made it to the door. My door's got dingy curtains and glass with some kind of grillwork over it, and at night you can see out without anybody seeing in if the hall light's not on. But in daytime they can see you too, and they did. There were two of them, both in dark suits, both tall, but one was blond and the other dark. They had the same look that the security officers at Boeing had: like they knew all about you and where you hid the body. Well, in my case, left it.

I opened the door a crack, and they drew. Not guns, I don't know if they're that practiced about that, but those thin leather folders with the badges and credentials came out in a way that reminded me of the gunfighters on TV. While they held them out, the one identified as FBI Agent Alessandro said, "Mr. Crane?" It wasn't exactly a question either.

I admitted to being Paul Crane. Hell, they might have arrested me for doing him in, too.

The other one, with a card saying he was a "Duly authorized agent for the Central Intelligence Agency," said, "Mind if we come in?" I couldn't make out the signature on his card, and if his name was printed on it I didn't see it. I couldn't figure out what he was there for. For that matter, I didn't remember the FBI being in on narcotics cases either. There was nobody else with them.

You don't keep the FBI and CIA on the stoop while you ask for their warrants. At least I don't, and normally wouldn't, and I couldn't see any point in acting abnormal. I didn't have to try to look surprised, so I was saved the trouble. I didn't have to act to get a puzzled tone of voice either. "Sure," I told them, "come on in."

I led them to the office. "You'll have to excuse my robe. I just got up."

"Up late?" FBI asked.

"Yeah." I didn't explain. I still wasn't sure whether or not to just tell them and get it over with.

"You rode out to Lathrop with Daniel Ackerman last night, Mr. Crane." This was the blond one, CIA. With their shoes on and me in my slippers, they were just taller than me. I perched on the drafting stool and reached over to plug in the coffee pot. It was still half full of yesterday's coffee. Then I looked at him. "Yes. How did you know? And what do I call you, anyway? I couldn't make it out."

"I'm Harry Shearing, Mr. Crane. Louis, would you mind leaving us now? I think I'll handle this one." He didn't look at FBI when he said this. The dark one looked at me for a minute, then started out. Just before he left he turned back.

"Sure you know what you're doing, Harry?"

"Yeah. Just let me see what I can get. See you tonight."

FBI left, and Shearing sat down in my swivel chair at my desk. This put me looking down at him from the drafting table. My desk faces the front window and the drafting table faces the double doors to the hall, so we both had to turn inward to see each other. I wasn't very keen to. The coffeepot started making its popping noises as it heated up.

"I'm not here to play games with you, Mr. Crane. I need some help and I think you can give it to me. Please remember that. I'm not out to trap you into saying anything, and you don't have to answer anything I ask, and I'm not warning you anything you say can be used against you. Except in very unusual circumstances I don't have any authority in the United States anyway, and law enforcement isn't exactly my business. There is one thing I want you to agree to before I start. Everything I tell you from now on is classified information. You had a Secret clearance when you were at Boeing, so I don't have to tell you the penalties for talking."

"You also don't have any authority to make me listen," I told him. "What is all this?"

"I think you know a lot of it, Mr. Crane. Would you rather I got Louis back in here? He does have authority in the U.S. Or we could even manage a couple of deputy sheriffs if you want. Better listen to me and see what happens."

The coffee was hot so I poured some. Shearing shook his head when I offered him a cup. I took a long drink, scalded my mouth, got that down, and said, "Understand, I don't admit to having any reason not to let you get your friend back in here, but I'm curious. Okay, it's classified. Shoot."

"Maybe I will have some of that coffee after all. Thanks." He took the coffee and sat down. "Last night there was some trouble out at Richmond Landing. A deputy sheriff and your friend Dan Ackerman were killed, and another deputy was shot. I'm not looking at you, so you don't have to look surprised unless you want to. Also, don't say anything. Let me go on. In addition to those two, four other men were killed." This time he was looking at me, and this time I did look surprised.

He went on. "Three of the others were smuggling heroin into the country. They had come ashore in a dinghy, and they were met by one of my men and two deputy sheriffs. I told you we don't normally have any jurisdiction in the United States.

"Somehow, a gun battle was started. My man was killed down near the water. Everybody else was shot up on the road. One of the deputies, the one that lived, was hit early in the battle, but managed to get to his radio car and call for help. The other one continued the battle until he was killed. The surviving deputy says his partner wasn't hit until just before a green radio car came to his assistance. He also swears that there were two men in that car. One was Daniel Ackerman. We haven't identified the other one, at least not for the record.

"Again according to the deputy, there was a continuation of the gun battle. Ackerman shot at least one of the suspects, possibly two, but certainly not three because the third one killed him instantly and was himself killed by being hit three times with 9 mm. bullets. It is interesting to observe that no 9 mm. weapon was found at the scene.

"After this point the survivor lost consciousness, so we have to piece together what happened from what we found. The man with the 9 mm. was apparently not hurt. At least we found no blood where he was last known to have been when the battle was going on, nor where he lost his dinner in the bushes. And he seems to have moved around. Among other things, he found the heroin and put it in the deputies' car. Then he vanished.

"There was another man there also, or at least we think so, because we don't like to think that the man with the 9 mm., who we assume was the second man in

Ackerman's car, carefully cut the throat of one of the surviving suspects. And that, Mr. Crane, is exactly what someone did."

It made quite a story. I found I was sitting there just holding my coffee, so I took another gulp. It was cooler this time. "You say, Mr. Shearing, that you don't expect me to comment. Why are you telling me all this?"

"Oh, I haven't finished yet. I just want you to see the situation. The police are going on the theory that two different men were involved besides those found at the scene. However, they could be persuaded to look for just one if Louis and I suggested it strongly enough to them. And Mayor Sundesvall could be instructed to cooperate with the police instead of saying nothing to them. But at the moment, the police aren't interested in the man with the 9 mm. They think he was a special deputy, maybe he was hurt a little, and wandered away in a daze. They would like to talk to him, but they aren't pushing it. They could, though."

I guess I had a pretty tight look on my face by then. Hell, this guy had me sewed up in three directions if he wanted me. Throatcutting, yet. And while I doubted if any jury would ever convict me, I was also sure that quite a lot of people including a jury would believe I had cut the throat of the other man in revenge for Danny. They'd let me off as justifiable, I figured, but that sure would play hell with my business. My whole life for that matter. I finished the coffee.

"Okay, Mr. Shearing. I see what you're driving at. Now what did you really come here to say?"

"That's simple. I came here to recruit you for the agency. We need some help on this mess and you're in a good position to give it to us."

"Wow," I said. I didn't put much conviction in it; he'd already told me he needed help and then hinted about how I might get arrested for all kinds of sordid deeds if I didn't cooperate. Still, it's a shock. I've read about the cloak-and-dagger boys, and for a while there at Boeing I even got to look at the results of some of their work—pretty spectacular, if you could believe it—but I never met one. One that I knew for sure was one, that is. Now it looked like Paul Crane was about to become a junior-grade spy himself.

"You mean you want me to become a spy, travel to exotic places, make love to beautiful women, pad expense accounts and . . ." I let it trail off. Harry Shearing was definitely not amused. "Okay, Mr. Shearing, what do you mean?"

He looked around my place. "I can't tell you all of it here, Mr. Crane. It's unlikely, but conceivable, that someone is listening to us. So far I haven't told you anything they couldn't figure out for themselves, or must have figured out if they know enough to wire your office. The rest of it I would prefer to tell you somewhere else."

"I'll get my clothes on," I told him, and went back to my bedroom. I didn't figure it was worth looking like Shearing already, so I put on slacks and a sport shirt. Let him wear dark suits all he wanted to, I'd had my fill of that in the aerospace business. Before we went out I put something out for Tiger, which was unnecessary. That cat could live if every human on earth dropped dead, except he'd have to train a chimp to scratch his ears. He'd do it too. While I was feeding Tiger, Shearing joined me in the kitchen and suggested the back way out. I let him out the back door, but it was a point for me. I mean, men in dark suits visit consulting engineers every day, but how many go out the back door?

He had an Impala around the corner, and we got in it. Louis was nowhere in sight, and I decided I might have seen all I was going to of the FBI. I hoped. We drove out to the Ballard Locks, which isn't a bad place to go. Ships come in and out; ships, and boats, and yachts, from all over the Sound and the world. They go into the locks, which lift them eighty feet from salt water to the fresh water of Seattle's big lake and canal system, and lots of them unload right at the business that's going to use their cargo. I could see how it made sense from Shearing's view too. Nobody could bug the whole grounds, and you could be in a position where not even one of those shotgun-parabolic reflector mikes could pick up any conversation over the noise of the water and boats. There's a kind of park that goes with the locks, and we found a bench and sat down to watch the boats coming in.

"Now what?"

"Now I tell you about what's happening around here, and you decide whether or not you want to help stop it. Look at these."

He was holding out some photographs of kids, young kids, maybe fifteen to twenty. Every one of them looked as though they were undergoing the tortures of hell. There were ten of the pictures, each one a different kid.

"Gets you, doesn't it?" Shearing asked. He pocketed the pix.

"What's wrong with them?"

"Withdrawal. The cure. You know, kicking the habit."

I thought about that for a moment. "That's the Treasury boys' job. Or maybe even the FBI. What have you got to do with that?"

"It's their job to stop narcotics. It's my job to stop the Red Chinese from building up their agent net over here. It turns out I have to do their job to do mine."

"Maybe you'd better run that one by me again."

He took out a pack of Camels and offered me one. "I'll start at the beginning. The Chinese have never had much of an agent net in the U.S., and mostly relied on getting information from the Russians, who have a very good system. But now it seems that the Russians aren't cooperating, so Beijing has to build her own or go without. The first thing you need to get a net going is money, local currency, and they haven't many dollars. They do have a lot of poppies. What's more natural than bringing in heroin and opium to finance their espionage? Dope takes up less bulk than money, and money's no good unless you have it where you use it. So they bring in dope, sell it, and use the money to recruit and pay expenses. Simple."

I thought about it for a while, and it made sense to me. "Okay," I told him, "I'll buy that. Now where do I come in?"

"What do you think they look for in an agent, Paul?" I noticed he had switched to my first name. "What would be ideal? It would be a man with an independent income of sorts, who has a job which lets him keep irregular hours; a man who travels a lot, is respectable, has enough technical training to be able to know whether something is important, and who has already been run through a security check but isn't working at present in classified areas. Add to that your ex-wife's political sympathies, and you have Paul Crane, consulting engineer. I'm surprised they haven't tried to recruit you already."

"But anybody in his right mind would know I wouldn't work for them, and anyway I haven't any training."

"Mr. Crane, they can't be choosy. The Russians have experienced cadremen here. Colonel Abel had been here twenty years. But the Chinese have to use what they can get. This is a big amateur show, Paul. As for why they might think they could get you, you have no known political opinions. I believe you pride yourself on getting along with everyone."

"Had to, with my wife around. Guess I just got in the habit of never arguing. If it means anything to you, I do have opinions on the subject."

"We know. We talked to your mother. But I doubt that they can or will check that far. However, your opinions are of no matter, Paul. If they want somebody bad enough, they can frame him for something and blackmail him. That's not the usual technique. The usual technique is to enlist his sympathy for some cause or movement unconnected with their real objective and get him to work for them in it. Then in something else. Finally comes something harmless but illegal. When he begins to get sulky, they let him have it: cooperate or we publish what you've been doing. It works more often than not."

I threw away the Camel, realizing as I did each time I lit one why I gave up smoking cigarettes. "Okay. I'm prime bait for them. What makes you think I'd be useful to you?"

"The qualifications I spelled out before fit equally well if you look at it from our side. We haven't unlimited resources, you know. The FBI has more men on this than I do, and they have a limit to what they can do, and I have the problem of hiding any trace of my office's involvement in domestic affairs. My people have to be just as careful to avoid our side as enemy agents do."

"Then what was the FBI doing at my house?"

"Louis is an old friend, and unlike most of his agency he isn't jealous of who does a job as long as it gets done. They got a routine report on this whole operation weeks ago, and we decided to approach you then. I take it Mr. Ackerman didn't mention anything to you."

"Danny? Good God, was he in on this?" Shearing nodded. "It begins to fit together. Hell, he knew about something going on at Richmond Landing too, that's why he went balls out when he got the signal."

"Of course. We learned that the stuff would be brought in several days ago, and alerted our people. Ackerman was one of our best, and he was assigned the job of getting on the Lathrop police force because it seemed he might be useful there. Being a policeman in a cornball town isn't as silly a cover for a counterespionage agent as you might think. Ackerman had a reputation for being rather lenient on politics and getting concerned only with violence and criminal disorders, and thus was able to be friendly with at least some of the student group here."

"How did you find out about the stuff?"

"As it happens, that's none of your business. A contact told us about it coming in at Victoria. The Royal Canadian Mounted Police saw it go aboard a small motorboat registered to a Mr. Lawrence Blevins. Mr. Blevins kept his boat at Richmond Landing and had made several trips to Canada, which made it reasonable to let him get here with it and see who met him. I sent one of my men and two deputy sheriffs down, because we couldn't get permission to let them bring that much heroin into the country. My man had instructions to use his judgment about whether to apprehend everyone or

let someone get away to see what would happen.
Evidently they were better than he thought they were.''

"I take it Mr. Blevins was one of the bodies."

"Yes. The short one. The one who had his throat
cut.''

"Can I think about this for a while, or do I have to
give you an answer now?''

"No. With the loss of Dan Ackerman I don't have
enough coverage of that university group, and I need
some now." Shearing took out another Camel, and I lit
my pipe.

I thought about this for a minute. I didn't see I had
much choice, much more than somebody who had been
roped in by the ChiComs the way Shearing described it.
Hell, I was roped in too. Then I asked, "That's twice
you've mentioned the university. Why?''

"Does it occur to you that there are not many groups
that keep weird hours, have no visible means of support, have contact with people who work at Boeing,
have some smattering of education, and openly sym-
pathize with China in the argument with Russia?''

"Yeah. It also occurs to me that that is about the
unlikeliest group of losers anybody in his right mind
would employ for spies. Hell, most of them wanted to
be Communists a long time ago, and the Party wouldn't
have them.''

"Their new friends can't be so choosy. I grant you
they aren't what the Chinese would pick if they had a
choice, and that most are harmless, but it's a start.
Somebody in that gang is the logical contact with you if
they want you; and before we're through they'll want
you.''

I watched a big ship floated up the locks while I
digested this. "First you've got me in a bind," I told
him. "And the way you say it, they'll soon have me in
one. Thanks, but right now I'm just suspected of cutting
throats. I think I'd rather have that than treason.''

"It won't last that long. These are amateurs, Paul.
They can't have many trained men. They're vulnerable.
They can't have a competent cell system or anything like
one, and they can't have enough men they trust to

manage the money. As near as we can figure it, they've got close to a million dollars out of this operation and they're ready to start spending it, but they really haven't much of an organization yet. Their whole operation is tied up in one or two top men, who will also have the money. I want those men and I want that money. All you have to do is find me one name. You or somebody like you; you aren't completely alone on this, but as I told you I don't have unlimited resources and can't recruit all the people I'd like to. Just find me that name."

"They may be amateurs but they aren't going to give me the name of the top dog in any short time."

"I never thought they would. But they might let you identify somebody who does know. You tell me who knows and I'll have the whole thing wrapped up in two days."

Shearing had a chilled look in his eyes, and it scared me. His whole face showed dedication. Hell, he reminded me of one of the student activists popping off about the war. "How?"

"You know as well as I do. This is war."

"I thought there was something called a Constitution in this country."

"There is. It protects rights. If it's gone there won't be any rights. It's my job to see that we keep it. Look at these again." He pulled the pictures out of his pocket.

I didn't want to look at them. Anyway, he even made sense in a funny kind of way.

"I sure have a choice, don't I. You'll ruin me, if they don't."

"If you like to think of it that way. I'd rather think you wanted to help your country."

"Yeah. That's all very well, Mr. Shearing, but I don't know what to do. Barring that funny business with Carole yesterday, I haven't had much to do with that crowd lately. It would look pretty suspicious if I suddenly sprouted leftist convictions and went around being friendly, wouldn't it?"

"By the time we're finished you are going to be so unsuspiciously attractive to that crowd that they'll stand in line to recruit you. Describe the funny business yesterday.'' Shearing got up and walked toward the locks, and I strolled along with him. He stopped at a coffee machine, we got some, and went to another bench. I told him about Carole's attentiveness as we walked, and also told him what Danny had said.

"You don't know that wasn't a recruiting attempt,'' he said. "Whether it was or not, it might help. Your connection with that group isn't going to be motivated because of political reasons anyway. Your story is that you're tired of square company and getting lonesome, so you go to a few parties with your old friends. While there you are going to offer them services, but they won't think you're offering. This Halleck business works right in. Make a play for her. If she's after you, let her catch you. We'll look her up, but if she's talking to John Murray, she gets word to everyone we need to reach. You see, I think Murray may be the man we want to talk to. I think he's up here to help set up the net for them.''

"Yeah. I'd thought of that myself. He's had more training than most of them, he's smart, and he has some standing in the left wing. Now what service am I going to offer them?''

"I haven't been trying to be mysterious, Paul. I've been trying to make up my mind about something, and I've decided to do it. You're going to help them bring in a shipment of dope. They'll have enough in reserve to take care of their customers for a little while, but last night hurt their expansion program and they'll be getting desperate. I'm going to tighten up the border, particularly for them, so they'll be looking for a new courier. You. But they wouldn't trust you with that, so they'll have to have a way of getting you to do it without your knowing what you're doing.''

"Even I can see what you're driving at now. I'm going to take a trip to Canada, and somebody is going to volunteer to come along with me.''

"Right.''

"But I still don't get it,'' I told him. "That border's wide open. You drive through and there's a joke of an inspection, and that's that.''

"It won't be a joke anymore. As of this afternoon, we'll run every license that crosses through the computer. Anybody who has any connection with this outfit will get a thorough search. We'll also have a random search of other cars. The customs people won't like this too much, but they'll keep it up for a couple of weeks, and by then our friends will be getting worried. They won't use a car to bring it down with that going on.'' Shearing seemed to be enjoying himself now. I could see he had put a lot of thought into his plan, but it still didn't make sense.

"Then how,'' I asked him, "am I supposed to get there and back with the stuff?''

"By boat. Tomorrow you are going out and buy yourself a sailboat. You used to have one, didn't you?''

"Sure. Had to sell it to raise cash for the divorce settlement with my wife. This job begins to sound interesting.''

"We'll give you money as a fee from a perfectly legitimate corporation. You'll buy a boat that you can sail to Victoria with at least four people aboard. Finance it at the Union Bank in the District. The girl in the Loans Department, Janie Youngs, will be your contact from now on. She knows about as much about this as you do, but not more. You will make your reports to her, and take instructions from her. Remember the name, Janie Youngs. She's a rather pretty blonde, so you won't have much trouble noticing her in the bank. There's not much more I can tell you about this anyway, except that if they do use you, you'll be carrying something pretty dangerous, so don't get curious. They probably won't let whoever they send know what's in the package, but once it's in the U.S. it has to get to the top pretty soon. We'll arrange to follow it.''

I whistled. A long, corny whistle. This thing was getting bigger, and I wasn't used to it. It scared me. I tried to sound matter-of-fact like Shearing, but I wasn't very good at it. "You're going to let heroin into the country? Help them get it in?''

"Yes. It isn't that hard to get in nowadays, anyway.

We'll clean up the whole organization if this works, and we won't have helped them as much as you think if it doesn't. Not that I want that stuff here any more than you do, but this is the only way I see that has a chance of breaking them before they get organized. At the moment they won't have many people, and they won't trust most of those they have. There's a very good possibility that the stuff will go to the top with only one link between your escort and the head. We just might be able to get it out of that link."

"You're the boss." We talked for another half hour about details, and he drove me to the District. I left him a few blocks from the house and walked back. It was quiet, and I got a beer and sat down in my office.

Nothing looked different from yesterday except I didn't have blueprints on the drafting table. Tiger came in and I scratched his ears and thought about it all. It was scary. It was also coming to me that I had killed a man the night before. That may not be a very big deal for some people, but it was the first time for me, and it bothered me. I haven't had much religion for years now, but the idea that you don't kill people was pretty deep.

I drank a couple more beers and went out. On my way to the District I stopped at a phone booth and called the number listed for the CIA in the book. A girl answered, and I asked for Mr. Shearing. He came on in a minute, as he'd said he would, and we exchanged some pleasantries I'd learned back at the locks. I didn't give my name, and he didn't ask. After I hung up I knew it wasn't an elaborate joke, but of course I'd known that before. The ID cards might have come out of cereal boxes, but they had my name and knew I was with Dan last night, which made them more than jokesters. Paul Crane was a real live junior counterspy.

4

ABOUT TEN THAT night I went to the Eagle Tavern. The Blue Moon used to be the big hangout for the rope-soled shoe set, and back when mostly they went there it was a fun place. At least I'd thought so when I was younger. But the owner threw some of them out for fighting, and others followed, and after a while the whole crowd shifted to the Eagle. They were nearly all there when I went in. I joined a table of younger guys I didn't know very well, and I hadn't been there long enough to drink a schooner when Carole came over and sat next to me.

"Hello, Carole. How's Jim?"

"How in hell should I know? I haven't seen him for a week," she told me. She was pretty huffy about it.

"I thought you made it with him."

"Used to be, maybe. No more."

I ordered a pitcher of beer and some glasses. This got the kids at the table interested, and pretty soon I found out one was an amateur military historian or something. He described in detail every battle fought before 100 B.C., and I got in an argument with him over the weapons used in the Trojan War. This may sound like a weird thing to argue about, but at least it was non-political and I figured to know as much about it as anybody else did. This is also the way the modern student spends his time. Drinking beer and having intellectual conversations.

Carole stayed right with me, which was a tell right there. No pretty young girl could possibly be that interested in old battles and Trojan armor. Not even for free beer. Of course it might be my handsome face, but if so, it's strange nobody else ever noticed it. Except my wife, and I wish she hadn't. Then Carole and the kid got in some kind of heated discussion over European literature. As the senior intellectual present, I didn't have to do anything but nod sagely and agree with one or the other once in a while, which is just as well, because I hate European literature. At least I think I would hate it if I knew anything about it. Oh, I read a book once in a while, but this existentialist nonsense, where all the characters in a book make speeches at each other while nothing happens, bores me. The conversation would have bored me except living with my wife had trained me to take this sort of thing. She did it by the hour. Anyway, I was a good listener.

Taverns close at twelve on Saturdays in Washington State, and as nobody is ready at that hour to stop enlightening himself, there are always one or more parties to go on to. The trick is to find one, as they're all at private houses. I asked Carole just before closing.

"There's an YPSAL party at Ron's houseboat, but it costs to get in. It's a fund-raising party. There's supposed to be a keg."

"I wondered where everybody was," I told her. "Why didn't you tell me? That keg's all gone by now."

"I didn't think you'd want to go. Want to?"

"Sure. And I've got a case of beer in the trunk of my car. We'll have to walk to my house, I walked here. Unless you'd rather I got the car and came back for you."

"No, let's walk. I've never been to your house."

"It's a good half mile up to my place from the Eagle, but she kept right up with me. My Barracuda was parked outside, and we got in. While I was warming it up she made the usual noises about it being a nice car.

"It's a compromise," I told her. "I sometimes have to take clients out to a site, so I can't have a sports car, but with the disc brakes and four-speed stick I can pretend this is one. It's a peppy little beast." I wound the car up and drove us to the Lake Union houseboat colony.

Houseboats are one of the nice things about Seattle. They're all pretty old and decayed, because the city is out to eliminate them if they can, so nobody puts money in them. The city wants to do away with them because it claims they pollute the lakes; their toilets aren't connected to anything. I'll be impressed with that argument when they stop the dozen or so bedroom communities on the other side of Lake Washington from dumping raw sewage into the system. Until then, a few hundred houseboats can't hurt much in a lake that big.

Ron Tawling's was one of the larger ones, but it wasn't big enough for the party. You could see they had strung some boards across to connect his back porch with the one next to him, and people moved back and forth. Ron was taking money at the door. There was a sign proclaiming this a fund-raising party, all donations to the Young People's Socialist Alliance, YPSAL for short. Ron is one of those brilliant failures who discourage me completely. He's been studying economics or something and doing very well, but somehow he's never finished. He's always going back, but dropping out before the quarter ends. For six or eight years now he's been making a living in old book stores, driving a cab, washing dishes, or just talking to people so they buy him drinks. He also blows his head off every night, and sometimes gets so drunk he forgets it's Saturday and won't be able to buy anything on Sunday. Those Sundays are the only time he ever sobers up. Yet he reads a lot and is pretty sharp. As I said, it's discouraging.

They wanted two bucks to get in. I handed Ron a five and walked past. I was pretty sure the extra dollar would end up in his pocket, and I didn't mind. Ron is one of the old crowd I can stand, as long as I don't think of his moral relationship with women, that is. Not that I give a damn about free love; Ron's problem is that he must not believe in it, because he keeps getting married, having a kid, and getting rid of the girl. It's happened four times now. The girls are invariably young students.

I once stopped four fraternity guys from beating Ron's head in for kicks, so in spite of what he calls my infantile politics, he likes me. I didn't stop to talk to him, though.

The sight of my case prevented comments about me. As I had figured, the keg had run out, and they were getting low on cans, so anybody bringing beer was welcome. I salvaged a six-pack for myself and threw the rest to the wolves.

These parties are unbelievable. Everything happens at them. People sit around, mostly on the floor, and talk about inconsequential things as if they're the most important events in the world. Or they talk about important things like war and atom bombs, but all they say are trivial things. I have never heard a brilliant conversation about anything important at one, but I'll admit there's enough intellectual talent around at any given party to have one. I think it's mostly that they're already locked onto their ideas on anything that matters, so the only way they can demonstrate their brilliance to each other is to talk seriously about something trivial.

Carole and I circulated around, and I noted that she stayed pretty close to me. We lit in a corner and three or four of the old crowd my age drifted over. One of them asked me how things were going, and that seemed as good an opportunity as any.

"Good. I've made so much money I'm going down and buy another sailboat. You'll have to come out with me after I get it."

Carole leaned over toward me. The buttoned shirt didn't give you much view when she bent over, but even so you could tell that there would be a worthwhile one if she had on the right clothes. "Are you getting a big boat?"

"Not too big. Four or five berths maybe. Just big enough for me to take a vacation to Victoria in a week or two."

Carole seemed interested, but no more than any girl who was out with a guy about to buy a yacht. Nobody else seemed to give much of a damn either. I opened another beer and we talked about Russian art. It was the general consensus that it was degenerate. I noticed that even I couldn't say any worse things about Russian art than they did, which was quite a change from my student days.

All in all I must have made my revelation to everyone in the room, one way or another. It wasn't hard to bring up in the context of what we were all doing with the summer. Just as I was getting sick of talking about the joys of sailing in the San Juans, I noticed John Murray was looking interested. He still hadn't spoken to me, and didn't, but I was pretty sure he heard my spiel. He also noted that I was with Carole. I let my rambling anecdote about the last sail I'd had up there trail off, and we got back to something else inane. I wasn't getting drunk, but I'd had enough in the Tavern and there to loosen up a bit, so when the singing started I was ready to join in. That stopped all conversation anyway, and went on for half an hour or so. Most of the songs had to do with the wonderful things that would happen when the old order passed away. They always did at those parties. But they're great songs. The conservatives ought to get some good ones like that, because as it happens, when it comes to songs that appeal to the younger set, the snake has all the lines.

I didn't figure to stay till the close of the party, and Carole agreed. It was hard to tell what was on her mind. As far as I could see, she liked my company and was having a good time. She was pleasant herself, so I couldn't complain. In fact, the only thing that bothered me was that I felt I was using her. Well, maybe she felt the same way.

As we drove off, I said, "Something to eat? Hamburgers at the Nasty Tasty?"

"Sure."

We drove on. As we got back over the bridge across the ship canal, I said, "We could stop at my place, and I'll cook something. I haven't had anybody around to cook for a while, and I feel the urge."

"Great. I still haven't seen your house."

We got there, and she was properly appreciative of everything. While we were eating, the subject of the boat came up again.

"Are you really going to buy a boat tomorrow?" she asked.

"I'm going to look. I have a pretty good idea of what I want, so maybe something will be done, like I might make an offer. Want to come along?"

"Yes. But I don't know much about boats."

"That's all right. You can learn. I didn't know a damn thing about them until I moved to Seattle, but there's so much water around I thought I was missing something, not learning to sail. So I learned and now I'm hooked. Better watch it or you will be too."

We finished and got up, and it was very still in the house. There was that feeling in the air that happens when a man and a girl are alone together. I still felt it was a little cold-blooded, but biology was taking over fast.

Carole was a little tense too. I took a step toward her, and sort of reached, and she took half a step toward me, and there we were. After a little while we went in the study and sat on the couch, and things went on some more. By now biology was in pretty complete control for me. Probably her too.

I broke it off and said, "If I'm going to get up at any reasonable hour, I've got to get to bed. Still want to come with me tomorrow?"

She nodded. Then she got up and we started back through the dining room to the kitchen, so we could get out. My bedroom door also opens off the dining room, and instead of going to the kitchen she turned in there. "It seems a little silly to go home and then come back, doesn't it?" she smiled. I went in after her and closed the door.

I don't know whether Jim Randall had been teaching her or not. Somebody had done a damn good job, anyway.

5

I WOKE UP but it took me a couple of minutes to get used to the idea that the bed had somebody else in it. She was lying there asleep, slightly turned away from me, and her hair was spread out around her head, and she was beautiful. It bothered me that she might have been sent here by somebody else. Then I remembered that she was there because I was sent out to find her. Well, you could make a lot of philosophical nonsense out of that if you wanted to, but it didn't seem too good an idea.

It was ten-thirty, and I had to get up if I was going to look at boats. Getting a sailboat out of the deal was one thing that made this counterspy bit look better, and I thought I had best do it before Shearing changed his mind. She woke up when I started to sit up.

"Hi," she said. She had a little girl look, like I'd imagined a new bride might look before I found out better. She started to sit up and the sheet fell off from around her. I put an arm out and she moved closer, and things went on from there. This time it didn't seem very cold-blooded at all.

After I got up and started the coffee, it came to me that I could get pretty fond of this girl. That didn't fit in very well with Shearing's plans, but on the other hand she didn't seem much like the type who'd be interested in helping Red China. I was putting some nice pictures together about that when I remembered her picture in the paper, demonstrating against the war. She was in with a group which periodically tried to stop troops from sailing out of Pier 91 for the Far East. Then I got quite an argument going with myself about that. I mean, these kids did think they were helping the Chinese, but that wasn't supposed to be the main purpose.

Main purpose or not, I couldn't help remembering what
Shearing had said just before he dropped me off. The
war wasn't going to be won in Asia. It was going to be
won right here in the U.S., because if people could get
convinced we shouldn't be in it, the Chinese could take
over without any trouble. How much was that worth to
them?

I decided it was easier to just do the job I was supposed to do and be done with it. It doesn't take any particular philosophy to want to stop the importation of
dope. If most of these kids knew where the money for
their anti-war demonstrations came from they'd probably get out too. The trouble is that a true believer can
always find a reason not to believe something bad about
his cause, and we couldn't prove a thing in court without exposing most of the counterespionage people in the
FBI. That was what was worrying Louis Alessandro,
and the main reason why he was letting Shearing in on
the situation. Shearing could recruit amateurs like me,
and maybe we could help get some convictions without
blowing Alessandro's people out of their cover. At least
that was the story Shearing told the FBI. From what I
had seen of Shearing he wouldn't let anybody get within
a mile of a courtroom, and I wondered how he'd convinced Alessandro he would. Maybe he hadn't. Saying
he would give the FBI a story they could use if things
went sour, and after all it wasn't their agency that might
get in trouble. The hell with it. My job was to find out a
name. That was tough enough without solving problems
of moral philosophy.

Carole was cheerful at breakfast, and afterwards we
drove down to the boat yards along Lake Union and the
ship canal. There are a lot of them, and at any given
time you'll find dozens of boats for sale. The limit of
twelve thousand dollars Shearing had put on, plus the
requirement that we be able to take cruises within two
weeks, meant that I had to find a used boat. I saw six or
eight I liked in the first two places we went, but none of
them reached out and grabbed me, so we went on.
Carole seemed very interested in everything and made it

a pleasant day, even though we had the usual Seattle clouds and spots of drizzle.

Then we drove down to the Aurora Bridge. There are a couple of little boat yards there, tucked under this high bridge. The lake narrows down to a canal just at the bridge, and this was once a very busy district in Seattle. Clusters of houseboats, decaying old mansions, new businesses, and boat yards where real sailors instead of clubhouse ones keep their boats make it one of my favorite places in Seattle. The sun came out just as we got to Doc Freeman's. Doc always has used boats, and even before we got down into his yard I saw what I wanted.

She was an old sloop rerigged to make her a masthead cutter. The "For Sale" sign said she was thirty-four feet long, but she looked bigger. There wasn't anything extreme about her; she was one of those boats built back when they didn't design to racing rules but just tried to design good boats. She'd be fast, and she carried a lot of sail. The cutter rig would be useful to let you reduce sail easily in the Straits, and that was important because it blows hard around Vancouver Island in the afternoons. There were four berths, one of them quite wide so that it could serve as a double. That's unusual in an older boat. The new boats have double berths because they're meant to be sold to people who don't know much about sailing; if you've ever tried to sleep in a real blow you'll appreciate narrow berths that hold you in one place. Still, for what I had in mind, this one looked like what I wanted. She was called *Witch of Endor*, and after looking her over I decided I wanted her.

It took three hours of dickering to get Doc to throw in the equipment I needed with the price. He had a certificate of survey so I wouldn't have to have that done. With some brokers it's still a good idea to have your own survey made, but not Doc. He's sharp, but if he tells you something straight out, it's true.

I finally got it arranged, signed an offer which Doc said he was sure would be accepted, told him I'd arrange my own financing through a bank, and Carole and I took her out. There wasn't enough wind to sail, but the little Gray engine was quiet enough for it to be a pleasant trip around the lake. *Witch* handled very well, and I knew I wouldn't have any trouble learning her likes and dislikes. We cruised down by the houseboats and I pointed out where the party had been to Carole. When we came closer, we could see there were still some people on the porch looking out at the water.

It isn't a good idea to try to put a boat in at a dock until you have some experience with how she drifts, but I tested the engine and the reverse worked very well, so I eased her up to the houseboat and tied alongside. Ron was sitting there drinking beer and offered us some. He wanted to look at the boat and after I made him take his shoes off he came aboard.

"Nice toy," he said.

"This isn't a toy," Carole told him. "Paul says he could sail it anywhere in the world."

I laughed. "What I said was that people have taken boats like this all over the world. I didn't say I'd do it."

"But you said you'd go to Victoria in her. Next week."

"That's hardly around the world. But I'm sure going to do that. I've been looking forward to this vacation for a year now."

Ron looked up the mast and down into the cabin and then sat with us in the cockpit. "Have any trouble with the fuzz sailing into Canada?" he asked.

"No," I told him. "Only time I ever heard of a customs man looking at a private yacht was once they looked to see if a friend of mine had liquor aboard, and then all they did was see if he had several cases. Just barely looked around the boat. George told me later that he thought they seemed more interested in admiring the boat than anything else. I suppose if you had some reputation as a smuggler they'd take the boat apart, but I never heard of a Seattle yachtsman having any real trouble at all."

"How long does it take to get there?" he asked.

"Oh, depends on the wind. With the motor, and if

you don't mind going straight through, you could leave at noon and be in Victoria the next night without any trouble. That's allowing for taking it easy and not doing anything stupid. It's not all that far, and by water it's a lot closer than driving to Vancouver and taking the ferry over.''

"Sounds like a nice trip." Ron jumped back over to his porch and got some more beer. It was getting on toward evening and I didn't own the boat yet, so we left in the middle of the second can.

Lake Union is really quite pretty in an ugly sort of way. People are always filling in some of it to expand their shore facilities and one of these days it will all be gone, I guess, and I'll be sorry. It's right in the middle of the city and you can see a good part of Seattle from your boat. The Space Needle with its super modern construction is quite a contrast to the old warehouses and docks by the water. Carole said she hadn't been out on the lake before, and we talked about how it was different from the way things looked from a houseboat.

"The lake's pretty," I told her, "and the Sound is nice too, but neither one of them is much compared to what you see after you get out of Admiralty and up in the San Juans. That's the nicest country in the world. It's always raining in Seattle, but up there, not fifty miles away, it's a completely different climate. The area around Admiralty has sunshine and wind all the time.''

She didn't say anything, and I didn't want to push it. I mean, it wouldn't have done to talk her into making the trip with me if all it was would be a girl going sailing with a guy, would it? We secret agents can't afford just to have a good time. At least not in a boat paid for out of the secret funds.

I got the boat back to Doc's and dropped Carole off at her place. She said she'd change and come to my house about eight. Nothing was said about where she'd spend the night, but it didn't look like I'd be alone. After I let her out, I drove carefully back toward my place. There wasn't any traffic, and I could be sure nobody was paying any attention to me. I parked the car near the house and walked over to the campus.

The University of Washington is Modern Gothic, which means that they used modern materials to make medieval looking structures. There are also some white marble buildings of a more classic design, and now they've built some Modern Ugly style glass piles. I liked the cathedral look of the old buildings, and I don't think the new stuff improves it at all. They'd be nice if that's all there were but when your library is a copy of a French cathedral, an addition made out of steel and glass just looks stupid.

I didn't recognize anybody, so I used the telephone booth near the library. Shearing wasn't in the office, and I didn't particularly like describing my relationship with Carole to somebody I'd never met, but he couldn't seem less interested. As far as he knew I was just a code name—"Larry"—and he didn't even know what I was working on, or said he didn't. I reported that I had arranged for a boat, let everybody in the District know I had one and would sail it to Victoria in a week or so, and that I was on intimate terms with Carole Halleck, relation to the target group unknown but suspected. I also reported that John Murray had seemed interested in a mild sort of way when I mentioned boat trips, and gave him a list of everybody I remembered at the YPSAL party.

There weren't any instructions for me, so I went back home. Going into the house I picked up the Sunday papers. I hadn't had a chance to read the papers since Friday night.

It was all over the second section. The story was that some dope smugglers had been intercepted by two deputy sheriffs, and a gun battle followed. The Lathrop town marshal responded to the sheriff's call for help and had managed to kill two of the smugglers before he was shot. The deputy got the other. No mention of any Lathrop deputy marshal, and not a trace of a dead CIA man either. That was what Shearing said would come out, and it was nice to see that he'd got that part arranged all right. The papers also said that the Treasury people were looking for the distribution organization, and there was quite a long feature article on the rise of heroin addiction among teenagers and college students. There wasn't a word about a tie-in between dope and Red China.

That bothered me a little. I couldn't see how the Chinese wouldn't know the CIA was involved and knew about their operation, so why keep it a secret? Why not let people know how the Chinese worked? It might keep some of the kids from getting involved in this. It's one thing to work for world peace, and it's quite another to help ruin lives with dope. But they didn't pay me for thinking about that, so I decided not to.

Carole came over at seven thirty, carrying a little overnight bag and some school books. I didn't say anything about it, and she left the stuff at the house when we went out to eat. We walked over to the District and I decided that since I was on an expense account we might as well eat good, so I took her to the Armenian's place. This was a rundown old wood building that had once been a bookstore owned by a woman who claimed to be a witch. Witch or not, she acted like one. She also had cats, three or four of them. Tiger had fathered a litter of kittens on one, and that made about nine cats, and maybe that's why she lost her lease. Anyway the place was taken over by a Finn for a restaurant. The witch told everybody she had put a curse on the man, and maybe she had, because not only didn't the place get much business, but the Finn had stepped off a ladder while trying to decorate, and broke a leg. An Armenian fellow took over from him, and he was doing all right.

On the outside the place was crumbling, but he had fixed up the inside with Oriental motifs, made arches out of the doorways and such, and dressed his waitresses up in harem trousers. He served good food. Being Sunday, we wouldn't have been able to buy any wine anywhere, but since the place was within a mile of the university it didn't have a license to begin with. The state legislature sure protects the students. Too bad most of them don't want to be protected. I never had.

I had told Carole we would be going there, so she was wearing a dress. She looked nice. Hell, she was lovely. She had a silver comb-like thing in her hair, and a little brooch, and stockings, and she looked good enough to take anywhere. I found myself wishing she dressed like that all the time, and that I was taking her out in a less cynical way. Anyway she was good company.

They had entertainment, folksingers. Folksingers in the District tend to be two kinds: the real authentic ethnic addicts who don't sing anything not made up by field hands or convicts, and the political set who want to teach the folk how to sing songs of protest. The political kind sing in coffeehouses, and the ethnics sing in the better restaurants. This group was pretty good, but I only knew one of them. Used to be I knew almost all of the folksingers around that were any good, but I hadn't kept track of the new ones. I can't sing, but I do like the kind of party where everybody gets half-looped and has a good time shouting in rhythm. The trouble was that the people who liked the kind of songs I did had a reverent attitude toward them, so if your voice was bad like mine you weren't welcome to join in. I guess that's one reason I went to parties where the political singers were: at least they didn't act like they were in Carnegie Hall.

We sat back and listened after our dinner, and people started coming in for coffee and entertainment. One of them was Roger Balsinger. I tried to look the other way so he might not see me, but he did, and came right over.

My thing about Roger had nothing to do with politics. As far as I knew, he was a real right-winger. He was also the worst bore I knew. Back when he was a student he used to hang around us for financial reasons. His folks were some of the richest people in Seattle, and I understood he had more rich relatives in California, but they had cut him off because they got tired of the way he wasted his time and their money. So he hung around with us, and you couldn't insult him enough to get rid of him. Roger had such a colossal opinion of himself that he simply would not believe there was anybody he knew that didn't like him. No matter what they said or did to him he made like they were kidding, and that included slapping him around if anybody ever had the heart to do it. Not many did. He'd never fight back. Somebody he hadn't totally alienated in his family had died a few years ago and left him enough money to live on, and he worked at an insurance office where his family had an interest, but mostly he was waiting for somebody else to die.

He didn't ask if he could sit down with us: it would never have occurred to Roger that anybody wouldn't be charmed by his company. He looked Carole over. I could see he was impressed.

"Hi, Paul," he boomed. "She's nice. Who is she?" Among his other good qualities, Roger is not only sure that he is irresistible to women, but also convinced that any guy should be glad to turn over his current one to Roger as a favor to a great guy. The fact that he has the lowest score in the district doesn't seem to have changed his views at all.

"Carole," I said, "meet Roger Balsinger, a real swinging cat. You're lucky to be here when he came in." No kidding. I really said it that way, and I wasn't particularly trying to be cruel. On the other hand, since he didn't react at all, it told Carole a lot about Roger, which was what I intended. "Roger, this is Carole Halleck, and she both came in and is leaving with me."

He grinned and started telling us about what was going on in the insurance office, and how well he was doing in it, and how if we wanted him to he could get us special rates. Luckily the singers started in before he really got going, so we were spared some of it.

When they finished, he actually remembered he was sitting with other people and that they presumably had lives too, because he asked how things were going.

"Not too bad," I told him. "I've got a couple of new clients, and the work's real low pressure. Don't have a thing I have to get done for a month at least."

"Do people pay you much money now?" he asked. It's the one thing about other people that does interest

Roger, money and how much they make.

Carole must have seen the wolfish interest, because she decided to do a little put-down of her own. "They must," she said. She used her best sugar-candy tone. "Paul's just gone out and bought a thirty-four-foot sailboat, and he's taking her on a vacation cruise to Victoria next week."

"Hey, that's pretty good, Paul," he said. The way he said it didn't make it sound like he thought it was so good. He turned to her. "Are you going with him?"

It was still for a moment, then Carole said, "He hasn't asked me. I've never been sailing and I've never been to Victoria either."

"I just got the boat," I put in. "Haven't had a chance to ask. Give a man a chance to do his own asking, will you?" I took her hand and gave it a squeeze. Before we could continue the conversation, the folksingers started in again, and even Roger knew enough not to infuriate everybody in the place by talking while they were trying to tell us about the Midnight Special. It's a favorite in the District, and just about everybody joins in on the chorus. There were enough doing it that it would cover even my off-key baritone. Carole, as I already knew, had a very nice voice. Roger never sang. Too undignified. After all, Roger hired entertainers.

When the song was done, we chatted about nothing much, and a couple of students came in. They were dressed in the usual black outfits that mark the University District peace movement. To make it certain, the guy was wearing a black beard, not combed, and they both had "Make Love Not War" lapel pins. I didn't give them a second glance, there are so many of them around. They don't much come into the Armenian's because of the prices, but after the dinner hour you can get coffee, and the folksingers were one of the better-known groups specializing in authentic music, so it wasn't too strange they'd turned up.

Roger almost blew his top. He started in on how they were a disgrace to the District and ought to be run out of the university, and how the taxpayers shouldn't have to put up good money to subsidize people like that.

This could get touchy. On the one hand, it would look funny if I suddenly started defending the peace movement, because both Carole and Roger knew I didn't ever have much to say about politics. At the same time, I was trying to get in with that crowd, and Carole was paying a lot of attention although she didn't say anything. I looked back at the couple Roger indicated, and said, "Hell, that's just Bill and Janice Sykes. They're so square they've been married to each other for years. The way Bill tells it, the war's immoral, and anybody who doesn't try to stop it is too. Far as I know, though, he's more than sincere about it. Actually it's kind of nice that there are people who act on their moral principles, even if you don't agree with them."

"Act on their moral principles!" Balsinger exploded. "It's close to treason, that's what it is."

"Come now, Roger," I said. "It's not wartime, so how can there be treason in opposing our involvement? Hell, man, when I see how many guys go over there, and how little we seem to accomplish, I wonder if we ought not get out too. Why keep feeding a company-a-day meatgrinder? We ought to win or get out, that's the American way to fight." This was as close as I could come to saying something that Carole could report favorably, assuming she was reporting on me at all. I was beginning to hope she wasn't.

Roger spluttered some more, but he did agree that the strategy used over there was rotten and we ought to go all out to win. We bantered it around a little more, with me talking about how it was no crime to have sincere misgivings and all that, and free speech, and such, until the music started again. We waited until the next round of songs was over, and managed to excuse ourselves. Carole had hardly said a word since Roger sat down, which isn't surprising since both Roger and I like to talk. It came to me that it was pleasant as hell being around a girl who didn't have to get in and compete with you no matter what you were arguing about. I hadn't had much experience with that kind of girl for years, my ex-wife having been captain of the debate team her freshman year.

Outside, she said, "Thanks. I didn't know you felt that way."

"Sure you did," I told her. "I will admit that I may have got a little interested in bugging that blowhard, but I don't think I said anything I didn't more or less mean. Maybe having you around broadens my horizons." I took her hand and we walked back to my house, just like the other couples in the District.

It was now almost ten. It was nice having her around, but I was still no closer to knowing whether she just liked my company or had something else behind her being there, so I set out to discourage her from hanging around. I figured that had to be done with some delicacy. I couldn't put her in the position of having to be too obvious if she was there to report on me, and yet I did want to get rid of her if she just thought of me as company. Well, let's say that I thought I should want to get rid of her. Inside I didn't feel anything of the kind.

I've had a lot of experience boring women. My ex-wife told me that constantly, and after a while I practiced it as the only way to get back at her. I knew one thing. If there's anything a girl wouldn't like, it would be being ignored for a drainage system. So I went to the office and started spreading blueprints out on the drawing board. Here she had gone and got all prettied, and we went out, and the second night we were together I worked on something incomprehensible to her that couldn't be all that interesting to me.

She wasn't easy to ignore. Not that she pushed sex at me, just the opposite. She sat down in a chair on the other side of the room and read a book, and she had sense enough not to say anything to me when I took a reading from the slide rule and then stared at the ceiling for a while. My ex-wife never could believe I was working when I got that blank look on my face, but of course that's when most real work is done. Damned if Carole didn't act like it was a very normal thing for a guy to take her out and then bring her home and forget her.

She made coffee and poured me some once in a while, and when I got up and went to the bathroom she gave me a quick kiss on my way back, and that was all. By eleven thirty I could feel her all over the room. I looked around and she was sitting there reading, but watching me over the top of the book. She saw me look at her and sat very still. We sat there that way for a minute, then I got up, and that was the end of the drainage system for the night. Afterwards, lying beside her, I still didn't know a damn thing more than I had, except that if bed conversation meant anything, we were in love. The trouble was I didn't really know if either of us was.

6

THE NEXT MORNING it was raining, which is usual for Seattle. Carole got up before I did and fixed some breakfast, and didn't wait for me to finish before she dashed off to class. I got shaved and showered and went out. It wasn't too far to the bank, so I could walk, and I went through the Pay 'n' Save Drugstore and a couple of other places that have front and back doors, getting something or other at each to make it look natural. Nobody was paying a bit of attention to me, and the bank was nearly empty. It was just after opening.

Janie Youngs was easy to spot. She was a tall girl, maybe 5'10", and she had blonde hair that hung straight down almost to her shoulders and then curled. Girls used to wear that hair style a lot, and I like it, maybe because that's what they were wearing back when I first got interested in them. I wish they'd do it again. It can't be more trouble than these elaborate upswept beehive things that look vaguely obscene, and although it must be more trouble than short hair, it sure is worth it. She was also dressed like a career girl, and if Carole hadn't got all dolled up the night before that would have been very refreshing too. As it was I couldn't help comparing them, which didn't improve my frame of mind at all. Either one would have done. In the months since my wife finally walked out for good—in contrast to the on-again, off-again show that went on for a couple of years—I hadn't met one girl I approved of. Now I knew one and was pretty sure I was looking at another, and with neither one of them could I get any kind of normal relationship. Normal emotionally, that is; the physical aspects of my relationship with Carole were quite normal and more than satisfactory.

Talking to Miss Youngs, I couldn't get her age. When you first saw her she looked like a big but very young kid. Then she put on the horn-rimmed reading glasses from her desk, and asked what you wanted and it seemed she was as old as I am. I settled for her being between twenty-two and twenty-eight, which still made her older than Carole.

I told her my name, and she said, "Crane? Have any relatives in Gainesville, Florida?"

"No," I replied conversationally, "all my people are around Schenectady." This established that we were who we each thought we were, and it came off in a very natural manner. It's just the sort of thing people might say. "I'm interested in a boat loan," I told her. She got out some forms, and we went through the standard loan application procedures. Since I had telephoned it all in the night before, I didn't have much to say to her anyway.

When there was nobody around, she said, "Have you been approached about your trip yet?"

"No. Carole obviously wants to go along, and I'll probably invite her, but first I want to try something." I explained the procedure I was using to bore the kid stiff if she had only a normal interest in me. I didn't go into details as to how it ended, but I said, "She hadn't brought up the subject of the trip again when she left the house this morning. Incidentally, Shearing said I should take you out, but in view of the situation with Halleck that doesn't seem like a good idea."

"Maybe that's just what will bring her out if she's been instructed to watch you. If it's just your charm, I would think that the sight of you with another woman would do the job nicely."

"And if it is just my charm, as you put it, I've just hurt a nice kid and fixed things up for my social life."

"Mr. Crane," she told me, "I couldn't be less interested in your social life. We have quite a lot invested in you and your contacts with that potential agent of theirs, and your personal relationships with a female peace marcher are of no importance to the mission. You will call for me tonight at eight p.m." She handed me a printed card identifying her as "Jane Youngs, Loan Department, Union Bank," after penciling in her home address and telephone number.

"Yes, Ma'am." If a look could kill somebody, she was fried on the spot. "Where will we go, Ma'am, and how shall I dress?"

She wasn't happy, but her expression didn't change a bit. Anybody looking at us from across the room would have thought she thoroughly enjoyed processing my loan application. Her voice wasn't pleasant, though. "Will you get it through your demented skull that this is an important operation and not a game? I don't want to go out with you, but I think it's highly advisable. And you damn well are going to look as if you were enjoying your evening. We'll go to a movie here in the District, and then somewhere where it might be presumed that we are engaging in sexual activities. I'll let you decide that. Your loan application will have to be approved by an officer, Mr. Crane," she went on as one of the employees came by. "If you'll come back after lunch, I think we can have a check ready for you. Wouldn't want you to miss that bargain." She smiled pleasantly. I managed to get some sort of pleased look on my face too, and stood up. She gathered the papers together, including the copy of the offer on the boat and the survey, and nodded, and I left the bank.

I was mad as hell, and did something I haven't done for years, namely went home and had a drink before lunch. This spy bit was playing hell with my life pattern, I thought. Not that most guys would complain. Here I was sleeping with one girl and was supposed to date another, equally attractive. I couldn't really complain about the Youngs girl, at least not as far as looks were concerned. The trouble was that I'm basically a one-woman-at-a-time type. The playboy image has always sounded too damn complicated for me. Maybe it had something to do with marrying young, and before that I hadn't really had much social life anyway; but I wasn't very enthusiastic about trying to handle two women all at once. Well, it was time I learned how. I understand

General MacArthur was engaged to four at one time at West Point, and had to get his mother to come and straighten out the situation. That wouldn't do me any good. My mother was in upstate New York, and anyway she'd never believe the situation I was in.

While I was drinking, Carole came in. We'd never exactly discussed it, but she acted like she was going to be a semipermanent feature of my life for awhile. At any rate she didn't bother to knock anymore. Why should she?

"Drinking this time of day, sweetheart? You'll be a lush by thirty." She laughed, but there was this little edge of concern in her voice. I liked it.

"Stupid client," I mumbled. "Damn fool doesn't know what he wants. I'm just trying to generate an inspiration. If I don't do this very often, it sometimes works."

"Oh." She came over to the kitchen table where I was sitting and kissed me. "Had lunch?"

I shook my head, and she started puttering around. I figured I might as well get it over with.

"Carole, I have to go out tonight."

"Oh, that's all right. Can I stay here?"

"I think you'd better not. Hon, this is a date I've had with the girl in the loan department at the bank. Made it last week. Saw her today about the boat, and it would have seemed funny as hell breaking it while I was doing business with her. So I didn't."

"Oh. All right." She put the sandwiches she'd made on the table, sat down, and we ate. Neither of us felt like talking, and she looked hurt. I wanted to tell her the standard junk, like this girl didn't mean anything to me, and that sort of thing, but that would have been too natural. She finished eating and went in the bedroom, coming out with her little bag and her books. She must have crammed like hell to get her dress into the bag, because she was still wearing the shorts and blouse outfit she'd gone to school in. "See you," she said, and went out the back. I felt like hell. I even felt like we'd blown the whole job too, because Carole was the only real contact I had going with that outfit. I poured another Scotch, sipped it, made a face, and tossed it off. Then I poured another.

Miss Youngs wasn't in when I went back to the bank later. A cashier had a check for me, and I went out to Doc's. I'd already found out by phone that my offer was accepted, so I paid for *Witch of Endor* and assorted gear, and got down to installing some of it. The old anchor I kept for a spare, having bought a new larger Danforth and fifty feet of chain shackled to a cable—a hundred fathoms, or 600 feet—of half-inch nylon line. When I put down an anchor, I want to know that the boat will stay anchored. I've been in too many sticky situations where anchoring would have solved all the problems. I also put in a radio direction finder, one of the little Bendix outfits, and replaced the compass with one I liked better. There were a couple of other items like some new running lines, and so forth. I also hoisted each sail in turn and gave it a more careful inspection than I had when I was thinking of buying the boat. They were all in good shape, as I'd already found out, but there was a worn spot in the main. It didn't seem to need a patch yet, but I'd watch it.

Witch was a lovely boat. She had room to stow all kinds of gear, and she was pretty well outfitted as she came. The old owners had obviously appreciated her. A toolbox with almost everything you'd need for the motor was built in next to the engine, and there was a place to stow all the woodworking and rigging tools I'd kept from my last boat. She was really what I would have looked for for myself, or at least what I'd have bought if I'd been wanting a boat and seen her, and she also fit the requirements Shearing had laid on me. It was getting past suppertime when I finished. Time passes quickly for me on boats. I had already arranged with Doc to get a whole set of the charts I'd need, so there wasn't anything else to do but go home and get ready for my big date with the Youngs girl.

I put on slacks and a sport shirt, and a coat—not the one I'd worn Friday night with Danny—and wound up the car. It was a little early, and I said to hell with it, and got out again. Let her walk, it'll do her good. She didn't live a quarter mile from the District.

Her apartment was in a new building, with a heated pool about the size of three good bathtubs, and a courtyard full of big splitleaf plants and redwood bark to discourage weeds. Instead of an inside hallway, it had covered balconies running along the inside courtyard, which meant that everybody in the place could see everything that went on in it. I knocked on her door, then again, and was about to worry when it opened.

She was all over me. "Paul, sweetheart," she started, and after that neither one of us could say anything. I found myself involved in a passionate reunion, which didn't make sense, but she was the boss. Then we broke it off, and she got her bag, and down the street we went.

"What in hell was that all about?" I asked her when we were well away from everybody.

"That was all about discouraging the boys who live across the court without letting them think I'm Lesbian," she told me. "You didn't mind, did you? It didn't seem like you minded." She grinned at me, and it took an effort to remember I was mad at her.

"That's all right, sweetheart," I said in the best unemotional tone I could manage, "but how about the job? If I'm supposed to let Carole woo me into being a Trotskyite, won't it look a little strange for me to have another true love?"

"That was the other reason for the scene. Paul, the love bit isn't good enough for this job. They won't trust it. Oh, sure, female agents manage to work the sex angle for information and even some cooperation, but you can never trust it to last. Besides, we haven't time to build a convincing case for you. The Halleck girl may actually get convinced that you're in love with her and will do anything she asks, but no supervisor, even an amateur, will stake anything important on her opinion. That's why you and I will be seen together two or three times in the next week. They'll believe you have a strong interest in sex, even if they don't believe you're in love. They can work it from there." She took my hand, and we walked toward the District. Like my wife, she didn't like to walk very fast.

Under the street lights I had a chance to look her over. She was wearing a skirt and sweater, and while she looked nice, she wasn't anything like as attractive as she had been in the bank. There was a little too much makeup, somewhat disarranged by our hello, and she overdid the walk a little. She did look sexy as hell, but I'd liked her better before. I guess I'm a sucker for the polished, well-bred type, and when that's not around the well-scrubbed outdoors girl. The nice thing about that is that it's possible for the same girl to be both.

The Varsity Theater was showing one of those incomprehensible foreign films in which everyone is miserable and makes sure he won't get out of the situation making him miserable. All the intellectuals have to see every one of these films, so we had a good audience for our own show in the balcony. Janie Youngs made it damn clear that everyone was expected to think we were headed for bed.

After the movie, we walked again, and I steered us toward the campus. When we were away from the theater crowd, she said, "The Treasury people report that that heroin was more important than we knew. The distribution people are having trouble getting enough to keep the customers happy. These people are either more incompetent than we thought, or they've hit a streak of bad luck by over-recruiting addicts before they had a backlog of drugs big enough to supply them. Either way it's a break for us, and it makes this plan a little more likely to work. Shearing thinks they'll get frantic for somebody to carry the stuff out of Canada pretty soon, but they won't want to take the risk with anyone important. You may get a new offer for company on that trip sooner than you think."

"After tonight," I told her, "if it's Carole I'll buy the idea that she's a messenger girl. There were three or four of her friends at the Varsity and they saw us. Hell, the show you put on, everybody saw us." We were on the campus itself now, walking under the trees. It's a nice campus at night.

"We might as well give them a little more if they're watching," she told me. We sat on one of the benches for a while.

The trouble with that sort of thing is that it's hard to act and keep it that way. At least it is for me. If I get that physical with a girl, I'd just as soon stop all the mental processes for a while and enjoy it. I got her up and we walked toward my house.

"At this point, you have a choice," I told her. "We can stop this show business and go hide in a closet or something for a sufficient length of time, or we can start it up and end up in bed. But I will be damned if I'm going to get that frustrated over anything, job or no job."

She looked at me with a funny little grin. "After the last couple of nights with Carole, I'd think you would be in a position to be more objective about it all."

"Why don't you lay off Carole for a while?"

"Because, Paul Crane, I'm as endowed with female emotions as anybody else, and I like to know how I compare. While you're on the subject of Miss Halleck, Shearing says to tell you not to get involved. I thought you'd be insulted by such instructions, but now I think you need them. She may be a cute little kitten, my friend, but she has been around. Did you happen to know she was one of the people sent to represent the University of Washington at a national conference of Stop the War leaders?"

"No," I told her. "I knew she was involved, but she gave me the impression that she wasn't very high up in the organization."

"That's one of the reasons we're interested in her. In fact, that was what decided Mr. Shearing on taking the gamble on you getting the stuff in. We think she may be a second echelon herself, although I doubt very seriously that she is aware of any connection between narcotics and the peace movement, or who knows who finances the peace business. But that innocent little kid friend of yours is a pretty effective leader, Paul."

"Okay, you made your point. What do we do from here?" We were getting close to my house.

Janie looked at me. With her height she didn't have to look up far. "Paul, just what do you think I am? Some kind of hardened superspy who seduces men for the good of her country? I guess I could do that if I had to, but mostly I happen to be a girl trained in business management who got recruited into this business because I could see that somebody had to do it. I've had more training than you have, but we don't have the kind of people you seem to think I am. If we do I never met any. I've been assigned to be your girl friend, which means that I'm stuck with you however you turn out, and it also means that until this is over I don't go out with anyone else. You happen to be a reasonably nice guy who I know more about than I do about anyone else in Seattle. I don't mind having a little fun with my work, but I'm damned if I'm going to get raped by my partner. With a little luck, though, our having to spend some time together doesn't have to be so bad, does it?"

"When we get in that house, Janie, we have to act like they're listening. Shearing told me that and I'm sure he told you. Before we go in, there's this one thing. This afternoon I was thinking that it would have been great to meet either you or Carole without all this other jazz. I still wish it had happened that way. But it didn't, and I was married for several years, and whatever was wrong with my wife didn't affect her sex life. Missy, I just ain't used to playing games. It's not part of my makeup. When we get inside, if you start in like you did out there on the campus, I'm apt to lose control. And after that I'm apt to want to justify it to myself by deciding I'm in love with you. What with already playing that game with myself over Carole, it could develop into quite a situation. Now let's go in."

As we started for the stairs, she said, "We're going to have this problem as long as we're together, aren't we? Let's get it over with and maybe you can be rational."

I took her home two hours later.

• • •

I spent all day Tuesday getting *Witch* ready and taking her out for practice. She handled as well as I'd thought she would, but that was Lake Union with the breezes we get in there. I still wondered how she'd take a real Juan de Fuca blow, but I wasn't worried.

Cruising down the lake I had time to think, but I didn't really want to. You can only think the same things over and over so many times, and every time it added up to the fact that I wished to hell I was out of all this. I wasn't used to using people, or to assigned company who had to like you whether you wanted them to or not. The spy bit didn't bother me; I could work up a real case of hate for people who sold dope to kids, and I wouldn't mind catching some Red Chinese agents. But here all I seemed to be doing was waiting for something to happen, and spending a good part of the waiting time in bed with somebody under rather strained circumstances. I kept telling myself I was crazy. Here I had two perfectly good chicks, both damned attractive and both amenable to seduction, and I had to worry my head off about whether or not it was genuine. Lots of guys would saw off an arm to have my troubles. On the other hand it couldn't last. If Carole didn't get back pretty soon, and in a way I was hoping she wouldn't because that would prove that it had been real, she was gone for good. And if somebody didn't proposition me shortly after that, Janie would get a new assignment. What happened to Paul Crane was something I couldn't figure, but I didn't think Shearing would toss me to the wolves. Not unless he could get some advantage out of it, and I couldn't think what that might be.

So after a while I gave up thinking and became a part of the boat. I ran up every sail, practiced heaving her to with and without the engine running, practiced getting the sails up and down, and got to know her pretty well. I still liked everything about her, and if nothing else in this crummy game came off I was going to keep her, one way or another.

There was a light on inside when I got back home. I

hadn't left one on, and I got a tight feeling. Which one was it? When I got inside, there was Carole in her shorts and black stockings, hovering over the stove, and saying, "What kept you? I've had dinner ready for an hour."

7

CAROLE WAS BACK, and I was glad to see her, but I had still been hoping she wouldn't be. After all, it looked like a good possibility that she had some reason to be there other than just an interest in me, no matter how unflattering that might be for my ego.

"Hi," I told her.

She started to say something, didn't, turned away, then looked back. "You can't get rid of me unless you really want to, Paul. I won't let myself be just a good lay. I think we mean something to each other, and I'm not going to walk out. You'll have to tell me to go this time."

She stood there with a defiant look, and I was right back where I started. Job or no job I was a good halfway in love with this girl, and I wanted to believe her. Hell, maybe there'd be somebody else take me up on my little sailing venture. Whether there would be or not, it was time to give them a chance.

We went to the Penthouse Theater after supper. The University of Washington has three theaters, all acquired by Glenn Hughes when he was head of the drama department. When he was in charge, they all paid their own way, with the university budget for his department being no bigger than for any other department of comparable size; smaller, in fact. Mr. Hughes made profits with his theater system, which is unique for college drama.

The Penthouse was one of the first theaters in the round, and had been a special project of Hughes. Most of the serious productions were put on there, with the showboat being reserved for money-raisers, and the playhouse alternating between experimental stuff and master's thesis productions. The play was quite good, a

Noel Coward comedy. After it was finished we went to the Eagle.

The usual crowd was there. There's something about taverns on the fringe of a university. They sort themselves out into different clubs. The fraternity set and playboys will go to one. Serious students of the liberal arts will patronize another, and the science and technology people generally find a third, although the engineers may, if the town's big enough to have one, go to a kind of less-expensive playboy tavern. But big or small, there will always be one more, where the students who take themselves but not their studies seriously, who think that what they talk about is vastly more important than anything else in the world, and who may even have dropped out of school years ago—where the rope-soled shoe set goes. It may not be a very big tavern, and I've even seen towns where there wasn't one for the serious students, but there will always be one for this outfit. The Eagle is Seattle's, and it draws customers from all over town.

The requirements for such a place are simple. The management has to abandon all hope of keeping order, although the customers will help him evade the laws about minors and fighting and such, because they'll know every inspector by sight from a block away. The physical arrangements should run to the shabby, because there will be fights once in a while, and although they won't last long and generally nobody will be hurt, they should be spectacular: which means some furniture should be broken. Movable chairs are therefore not too good an idea. Built-in booths are much better, and if made out of cheap plywood they are ideal. The booths ought to be laid out so there are several, but set so everybody can see everybody else if he wants. It should also be possible to tell at a glance from one central place just who is and who is not there. This saves trouble. There ought to be a jukebox, but the selections on it should be toward the unusual. Finally, there ought to be smooth easy-to-write-on walls in the men's room. Some of the finest doggerel and pornography in the world is to be found on the walls of the men's room in the Eagle. The crowd resents outsiders contributing, though, and will remove anything they think isn't clever.

If you have all these characteristics, and you are near a university, seriously consider turning your bar into a gold mine. It will be one, because there will be people there all the time. There will be a lot of deadbeats and you'll get your share of unpaid bills, but not too many. Late yes, but unpaid no, because ostracism from the place is tantamount to death for a real member of the group. They go there every night and stay until it closes, and on weekends you'll get tourists—come to see the beatniks.

That is what the Eagle is like. We sat in the front room, where the booths are padded and have plastic covers. You can have that in the front room, because your bartender—who presumably is the toughest stud you can hire—can watch them. Pretty soon we were joined by three or four of the crowd, and somebody got out the dice cup. The game this month seemed to be 4-5-6. It alternates. Sometimes they play 26, sometimes poker dice. I didn't figure 4-5-6 would last too long because the action is fast, and somebody generally gets cleaned out pretty soon. When everybody's cleaned out, there's nothing for the dice addicts to do, and they either have to loan money to the losers—a redistribution of the wealth—or invent a new game that takes longer. I played without getting involved and waited for something to happen. Nothing did.

For three days Carole stayed at my house, and we went to the Eagle, or to parties, or just around the District. I became friends again with some people I had lost track of, and I seemed to be getting some acceptance with the non-student crowd, helped along by my willingness to buy the beer, but nobody mentioned narcotics, espionage, Red China, or sailing to Canada. I did hear a couple of guys discuss why the price of Bennies was up, namely the fuzz were big up at the border, but that wasn't meant for me.

Friday rolled around, and I decided that I had better get this sailing date set. Friday night I picked Janie Youngs up in my car and drove her through and out of

the District. I hadn't told Carole, and I tried to look fur-
tive about it, even cautioning someone not to say
anything to Carole; I could be sure she'd hear about it
one way or another.

There wasn't anything significant said. I reported on
who was doing what in the District, which didn't
amount to much. I was given a key to a locker in the bus
station, from which I could pick up some gear I might
be able to use, including a gun. I was also told that
Carole was our best bet if anybody was, but to keep
looking.

I got back to the house late. Carole was still there and
she didn't say anything. We talked about the play we'd
seen Tuesday, and drama in general, and went to sleep.
If she'd heard anything about where I went, she didn't
mention it.

So Saturday afternoon I asked her if she wanted to go
on this trip. It didn't look like anybody else wanted to
come with me.

"I've been wondering if you'd get around to asking,"
she said. Then she kissed me. The job had its rewards
anyway. I set the sailing date for the next Wednesday,
and she decided to go immediately to her room and get
the clothes she'd need. "If I bring them over now, you'll
be able to see if I have everything I need," she told me.
She skipped out the door and I got busy with provision
lists. I could see her going down the street, looking
happy and excited and like a young girl again. I liked
her that way. I wasn't used to having her so damn serious about everything when we were alone.

We went to Eileen's for dinner because neither one of
us felt like cooking. While we were waiting for them to
serve us, Carole waved at some people coming in and a
young couple came over. They were about twenty-three
or so, the guy maybe a little older. He was clean shaven
and wore what looked like army suntans and a white
shirt with the collar open. He had short blond hair, and
stood maybe five ten. The girl was pretty well matched
to him, about Carole's height, medium-length brown
hair. In other words, they looked like perfectly ordinary
seniors or graduate students, which was a change from

the people I'd been seeing the last few days.

"This is Nancy Snow," Carole told me. "And Dick Wahlke. Nancy used to be my roommate last year, but she didn't come to the parties, so I guess you never met her."

I shook hands with Wahlke. He had a firm grip and looked at me when he talked to me. As I said before, I noticed these things after the last week. They sat down with us and ordered.

"Nancy, guess what? Paul's bought a sailboat and we're sailing to Victoria next week," Carole bubbled. I thought she was overdoing it, but what the hell. If it made her happy to act like she was in on the biggest thing since the Odyssey, why not let her? I guess there was a time when crossing open water in a sailboat would have excited me too. It still does, for that matter, but not that much.

"Gee, that's great," Nancy said. "We were up there last year. Took the ferry from Vancouver. It's sure pretty in Victoria." The girls fell to discussing what Carole absolutely couldn't afford to miss on the trip. Dick looked at Nancy, decided not to get in the hen game, and said, "What kind of boat do you have, Paul?" It sounded as if he'd thought of a way to work the sentence so he could use my name. That way he'd remember it, just like he'd been taught in Speech 101.

"She's an old sloop, one of those all-purpose racing-cruising hulls they used to build. Few years ago somebody re-rigged her to a masthead cutter. Thirty-four feet, but with the new rig I can handle her by myself. I expect that's why she was changed over, the main must have been a little big for one guy when she was designed."

"I used to do a little boating," he told me. "But it was all on powerboats. Went sailing about one time in my life, I think they called it a Snipe. Little centerboard job. Fellow took me out in the Sound one day when it was blowing good, and I got as soaked as if they'd towed me behind the boat. Scary too. Does your boat tip like that one did?"

I laughed, but made it friendly. "No, *Witch* has a

keel. Big heavy lead thing. In a centerboarder you have to lean out to balance the wind pressure on the sails. In a keel boat the keel does that.''

The waitress brought our dinners, and we stopped the conversations while we ate. Over coffee, Dick told me stories about the psychology department and a couple of kooky profs he had, and I regaled him with tales of my undergraduate days. After a while they left, and Carole and I had another coffee.

''They're nice people,'' I told her. ''Didn't know you knew any.''

''Aw, that's not fair. Anyway I thought you liked my friends. We've seen enough of them lately.''

''Sure, hon. But it is nice to meet somebody who likes to talk about something unimportant once in a while. I can't get used to saving the world every day. Besides, it needs saving from so much.''

''It does, doesn't it?'' She was smiling, but she was getting quite serious now. ''Paul, I wish you could see some of the films of what we're doing over there. They're hard to get because the government won't let them in the country if it can help it, but they're horrible. Villages blown up, little kids burned with napalm . . . I wish you'd look at some.''

''Sure. Got any around? Not that I really want to see them, but if it moves you that much maybe I ought to.''

''We don't have any right now, but there'll be a feature length movie on the war here soon. I grant you it will be films made by the other side and they probably slant them, but then so do we with the ones you are allowed to see.''

''Is it really that bad, getting the films?'' I asked her.

''Oh yes. John Murray was arrested in Sacramento for showing one. He's out on bail now.''

''Maybe he's right when he talks about police harassment. Most of the policemen I know would take a dim view of that sort of movie all right, and some of them might decide to do something about it, Constitution or no Constitution.''

''Well,'' she said, ''I think he overdoes it the way he tells it, because I don't really think he's as important as he thinks he is, but he's had enough experiences with police to be justified in seeing one behind every tree."

I thought of what I was supposed to be doing and how close she was to being right, and finished my coffee. "Come on, Carole, let's get some fresh air."

I wasn't really up to the blasted party, but we went. This one was like any other, except that it was at somebody's house, and the neighbors began calling the police about the noise at eleven thirty instead of waiting until midnight. The third time, the police were getting annoyed, and I decided we ought to go before they came in and maybe something ugly developed. Nothing noteworthy happened at the party anyway, if you don't count two pacifists getting drunk and taking a swing at a guy who preached anarchy and thought a little violence would be good for the movement. I didn't much blame the pacifists, I'd have taken a poke at him myself if he'd been shouting at me like that, but of course he'd scored his point by getting their goats.

Sunday afternoon I told Carole I had to drive out to see a client. Just to make certain if anybody followed me, a meeting had been arranged in the home of a retired colonel who lived on Queen Anne Hill. He showed me to his study and got out of the way. Shearing was there.

I reported the complete lack of enthusiasm anybody had shown about my upcoming trip.

"Well, the girl may be something," he told me. "They should be feeling the effects of our search pretty badly now. She could be the delivery service. I'm inclined to agree with you that she's not, but we've invested this much in the operation now, so carry it off." Shearing paced the floor while he told me this.

"Something wrong?" I asked him.

"Quite a bit is wrong. The Treasury people and the state cops want to move in on what we have of the distribution organization before they hook any more kids. Even Louis is getting nervous. He's managed to talk them out of it for a little while more, but I'm worried about him now. We've got to get some sort of break or I'll have to start over."

I lit my pipe. "Mr. Shearing, I don't know much about this, but couldn't you get something from the pushers? Like who they get the stuff from?"

"No, on two counts." He held up one finger. "One, they use dead drops mostly, so the pushers don't know themselves. I might be able to trap somebody by rigging something with one of the drops, but two, I don't dare let anybody but Louis know I'm in this. Paul, I have to level with you. If they ever got public proof that the CIA was messing around with internal security affairs, it would be one of the biggest propaganda hauls the other side could make this year. It would get Congress interested in a new watchdog committee, and hamper half my operations. That's why you haven't anything that could be used to prove a connection with us. It's why I have to turn to amateurs like you. I don't have an unlimited organization here. You'd be surprised how small our Seattle section is."

"I'd think Seattle would be pretty important, what with Boeing and all."

"It is. That just shows how careful I have to be. Anyway, you can see why I have to have people like you. That university crowd is prime material for the other side to use, but I have to keep my pros for their real organization. What few I have, and what little I know about it. Damn it, I have to find out who links the dope racket with the espionage group. It may even be the same one who runs the agitprop stuff."

"Sounds like the city is swarming with Chinese agents."

"Not really." Shearing sat down at the colonel's desk and took out a sheet of paper, but he didn't write anything, just doodled while he talked. "There are three basic groups. The biggest is agitprop. You know, pickets, anti-war propaganda, demonstrations, that kind of thing. It's the biggest operation they have, but there won't be more than one or two who know where the money comes from. There may be another two or three who know what country really runs the show, but not the names of the control people. These will be the ones who organize crowds, see that debates come off right by spotting people through the audience, the leaders. The rest are just people who agree with whatever cause they're supporting this time.''

He drew a hangman's noose, then somebody in it. Then he started putting spears through the hanged body, and went on. ''The next part is standard espionage. It may overlap with agitprop in order to make use of any information that it can get, but mostly it will hide any connection with obvious sympathizers. It will also be in the blackmail and recruiting business. This is the one they're trying to get going now, and the most expensive branch. Some people will be moved over from agitprop to it as the propaganda takes effect, but a lot of what they want will have to be bought.

''The third part is the money-raising section. Its size depends on the number of customers, but most of its people won't know anything about who they're working for. It will look like any other dope racket. We're working on it now, and the Treasury has a couple of informers, but we just don't get much. Now, somewhere, the money has to go across from this branch to the other two. It may be the same man in both cases, because they won't have too many they trust with that kind of dough. He'll also have files and such things, and accounts, because they have to have them. That's who we want. Now all I have to do is find out who would know. Once I know that, we'll get information, and Louis can have his commendation.''

''Yeah. Well this is an expensive trap. Thanks for the boat ride.''

''Don't worry about it. It's their money anyway. We took one of these operations apart in Sacramento last year. Nobody to return the money to, so we kept it.''

We discussed communications methods I could use in Victoria, and tried to dream up a plan that might work in case the boat trip didn't turn out to be anything else, and I wrote him a receipt. Shearing had decided to use this method to give me the money instead of letting me in on one of his dummy corporations.

I spent the next couple of days waiting for something

to happen. The whole business was getting to be a drag, because nothing did. Carole and I got to know each other pretty well, and I was still wondering if I was falling for her, but the whole idea that she was anything other than a nice kid involved at the outer edges of the agitprop group got sillier all the time. Either she was the contact, which I didn't want to believe, or nobody was going to take the bait. Shearing had told me he was trying a lot of stunts and most of them wouldn't work, but I hated to think I was just wasting time. I mean, what with messing my emotions up and all, the least I deserved was some of the action, wasn't it?

Tuesday night we got all the stores aboard *Witch*, and Wednesday about eleven in the morning we cast her loose and motored down the canal to the locks. For once it wasn't raining in Seattle. That's one thing about Seattle, when there's a good day it's a really good day, like nowhere else in the world. The Olympics stood out across the Sound, and back of us were the Cascades towering over the city. Usually you can't see either range, but after a rain, when the sun comes out, they're worth all the bad weather you had to put up with and then some.

We eased into the locks and tied up alongside a fishing boat, one of those sturdy forty-foot jobs you see all around Seattle, headed for the Pacific Ocean about a hundred miles west. It's always easier when you can tie up alongside somebody else, because then you don't have to fend off from the slimy concrete sides while you let 80 feet of line out to keep you from drifting into the current. The currents in the lock are quite strong, and when you reach the bottom and they open the gates, it can be tricky.

The locks are free, but you have to fill out a form that tells what boat you are, how many aboard, and where you're headed. I didn't have any of the forms aboard so the tender had to go get some, and I put the others in the cabin. The lock tenders take the filled-out forms, and they must do something with them, but I never heard what. Probably use them to justify bigger appropriations next year.

Once out of the lock, you're in the Sound almost immediately. We motored out behind the fishing boat until we were well clear of the traffic, and I headed *Witch* up into the wind. Carole steered while I raised the sails. It's not hard with the motor to keep steerage way, but without it, any wind can make hoisting a sail a bad job.

The wind was from a little north of west, which put it forward of the beam when I switched off the motor and got on course. It was blowing maybe fifteen knots, which can pile up a sharp chop for the boat to plow through, and worse, the sea was from dead ahead, out of Admiralty Inlet. The Inlet is about 15 miles north-northwest of the locks, and it takes you north and west 20 miles to the Straits of Juan de Fuca. You officially enter the Straits when you round Point Wilson, and then you have 35 miles of Juan de Fuca to cross to reach Victoria on Vancouver Island. The Straits of Juan de Fuca are named for an old fraud who, as I understand it, never saw them but took credit for what some of his captains discovered. They're formed by the Olympic Peninsula, U.S.A., on the south, and Vancouver Island, Dominion of Canada, on the north, and they connect Puget Sound where Seattle is with the Pacific Coast where nothing and nobody lives. Out on the coast you have the Indian village of Neah Bay where they don't even sell beer, and a lot of rock and hills. It's wild country. Most people seem to think Seattle is on the coast, which comes from school geography books having maps so small you can't see anything on them. As a matter of fact, the roads on the peninsula are so bad, most Seattlites have never seen the coast.

In spite of the head winds, it was lovely sailing. The sun was out, the mountains showed clearly on both sides, and we had the kind of weather Seattlites stay in our miserable climate for. If you don't live here, you can't understand why we'll put up with the horrible weather most of the year unless you get out on a good day like we were having.

It had taken more time to get everything stowed and get under way than I had figured it would, so it was well past one when we began sailing. With the wind ahead of us and the sea and tide against us we didn't make very good time, probably not over four knots over the bottom. Came supper time, Carole got the little gimballed alcohol stove going after I showed her how, and tried to heat something up. She soon found out why I had bought two little pressure cookers for the boat. Pressure cookers not only cook faster, they have watertight lids that won't come off when the pot rolls into the bilge. She had to stick her head up in the wind three or four times to keep the cooking smells from getting to her, but she didn't get sick. I don't get seasick in less than a real blow, and this was pleasant sailing.

There was the usual quota of pleasure boats out on the Sound, but they were mostly as big as we were. The wind and sea was just too much for most of the small sailboats that usually dot the Sound, but we passed two guys in a little twenty-foot sloop, a real beauty of a boat but small for my taste. They were headed for Admiralty Inlet too, and as we went by to their leeward I called out, "Headed for Victoria?"

The man at the tiller waved and shouted, "No, all the way down. Monterey."

"Good sailing," I told him. Carole had got everything on the stove tied down, and was sitting in the companionway. "Isn't that a tiny little boat to be going that far?" she asked.

"Yeah," I told her. "But the boat will be all right; that kind of boat will take you farther than you want to go. Whether the guys will go nuts from cramped space and the pounding they'll get out on the Coast is another story. Some people will do anything for laughs, I guess." Actually, I envied them. Not enough to change places with one, you understand, but still there's something great about taking a tiny little boat out in a big ocean like the Pacific. One of these days, I thought, I'll take a little bigger one—the *Witch* maybe—down that route myself.

It was great sailing. The sun came down, and a big yellow-gold moon came up, and the wind started to fall off. I taught Carole how to handle the tiller, and rested in the cockpit. I could see she was getting tired, which didn't surprise me. She hadn't done any work, but there's more effort required to sail than most people think. The boat pitches and rolls with the sea, and if you sit erect you have to keep adjusting your weight or you'll fall over. Do that for a couple of hours, and you've had a workout. When I do any sailing at all, I stop worrying about how much I eat, because I always lose weight.

After a couple more hours the wind fell off, and I knew that by midnight there wouldn't be any at all. I couldn't see any point in hurrying, and it was far too nice a night for that damn noisy motor, so I took over and brought *Witch* to the south coast of Whidbey Island. It's shallow there, and although there is a strong tide you can anchor if the weather's good. I got the small anchor out and dropped it, and tied the sails up so we could raise them in a hurry if we needed to.

The wind was just about dead, and the island protected us from any sea that might be left over. There weren't any clouds, just that bright moon and little ripples in the water. Living in a city, you forget just how many stars there are until you get out away from the lights and haze. We sat in the cockpit and smoked, and had a glass of Cointreau, and enjoyed the night for a while.

When we went below I was grateful for the unknown owner who had put in that double bunk. There was only one thing wrong with the night—the point on Whidbey we were anchored off was called Double Bluff. Somehow it was just too damn appropriate.

We made a dawn start but there wasn't any wind until after noon. Then it started to come up. I let Carole take over until it got stronger, but when I offered to take the tiller she didn't want to quit. I let her steer until the wind backed around, but finally it got almost dead aft.

"Better let me take it, Carole," I said.

"Oh, why? I'm not tired, and this is fun. It's really great, Paul."

"Yeah, I know, sweetheart, but it could get tricky now."

"I don't see why. The wind isn't as strong as it was

yesterday when you let me steer."

"Yes it is. It's coming from behind us, so it doesn't feel as strong, that's all. See, when we go into the wind it feels like there's more wind because you add the boat's speed to the wind speed to get what you feel. When we run away from the wind, the boat is going fast enough to make it feel like there's less wind." I took the tiller, and she moved forward a little, still sitting close to me. "Then there's this." I pointed to the boom. "If you steer too far away from the wind, it will get on the other side of the boom and push it right across the boat. If you happened to have your head sticking up when that happened it would probably tear it off. Even if the boom didn't hit anybody there's a chance it would slam across so hard it would dismast the boat. Running downwind seems real easy, but it can be dangerous."

Witch tore across the water. It doesn't feel like you're going fast, running downwind, because you don't get the wind in your face, but that's the best point of sailing for a lot of boats. It seemed to be for *Witch*. In an hour or so the sea really built up, and the wind got up to 25 knots, and *Witch* would surf down the face of a wave, almost tearing my arm off as I hung on to the tiller. She had too much weather helm, and I couldn't seem to balance it off with the foresails for quite a while. I finally got everything sheeted properly, and it started being fun again.

We made Victoria before dark. It took until after the sun was down to round the twists and turns of the channel, but there was still enough light to see when we tied up to the visitors' pier in downtown Victoria. They have a very nice facility for visiting yachts, in a protected harbor, with a view of some of the best parts of the city. It's in walking distance of the Empress Hotel, and the Parliament Building, and most of the downtown stores, so there's no reason why you shouldn't stay aboard your boat if she's big enough.

Carole cleaned up the visitors' facilities while I reported who we were to the harbor master, and then I shaved and showered so we could eat ashore. When Carole first got off the boat she could hardly stand. It usually gets to me at first, too. Once I took a five-day trip out to Neah Bay at the Pacific Ocean end of the Straits of Juan de Fuca, and when I got off, the land moved around so much I almost fell off a dock. Land-sickness is not a myth.

We ate at one of the little restaurants that you find all over Victoria. They're just like the guidebooks tell you about for London or any part of England, and they specialize in steak and kidney pie, a favorite of mine, or roast beef with Yorkshire pudding, and that sort of thing. Victoria is really more English than most of England. We walked around looking in the windows of closed shops, and dropped into a pub that had a ladies lounge—many don't. In Victoria, even where they do allow ladies, they can't come in through the same door as the men. It may be a bit Victorian, but it's better than trying to pretend that women are just soft men. I like customs that emphasize the differences. Maybe that's why I like girls in skirts. But then, I like kilts too. I decided to buy one the next day. The Cranes are lowland, but supposedly the name is Britonic-Celtic in origin, which doesn't really mean anything except that if you look hard enough you can find a tartan to match the name. Come to think of it, in some of those shops, if you look hard enough you can find a tartan to match any name you come up with.

Before we set out for our great expedition the next morning—we were going to take a tour to Butchart's Gardens, which you have to see if you go to Victoria—we had a second coffee on deck and watched the harbor traffic. Victoria is a busy port for being on an almost uninhabited island. Wakes from passing boats rocked *Witch*, not too hard, and splashed against the pier, and the morning was bright.

"Paul," Carole said, "I—well, thank you for bringing me."

"Sure, sweetheart. It's a lot more fun with you along."

"I've had fun too. I—will you promise not to get mad if I ask you to do something for me?"

"That's not too bright, hon. If it's going to make me

mad, getting my promise in advance not to do something I can't control won't help."

"Yes, but please," she said, taking my hand, "try not to get mad, will you?"

"Sure. I'll try."

"I'd like you to do something for me. You remember we talked about films of the war and how hard they are to get into the United States?"

"Yes." I got a whisper of an electric shock up my backbone.

"Well, there are some in Canada. I know how to get some. Can I take a few back with us? It will be smuggling and illegal, and you could get in trouble, but will you do it for me? You said you'd watch them when we got some, and this may be the only way we'll get them."

I kissed her. "Carole, sweetheart, you don't know me as well as you think you do. Hell, smuggling's no crime, I don't care what the sovereign people say about it. As for your propaganda films, if you think they're honest enough to show, that's good enough for me. Where do we get these lurid scenes of American atrocities?"

She laughed, more with relief than at my graveyard humor. "I have to call somebody this afternoon. You know, I think I love you, Mr. Crane."

"I thought we weren't going to say things like that, except maybe when we couldn't help it. Come on, kid, before I carry you below where you can prove it."

She stood up and kissed me, then said, "How do you know I don't want to do just that?"

"Time for that later. Although I will admit it could be more attractive than Butchart's Gardens, we didn't have to come all the way to Victoria for just that."

She laughed again, and smoothed her skirts out. "Yes," she said, "but you'll have to admit that the motion of the boat adds a certain something. Let's go."

The gardens were lovely, and indescribable. Every conceivable variety of blooming plant and color is blended into that place, so that it makes your eyes hurt to look at it after a while. We ate lunch in a little outdoor pavilion there, with a view of hills covered with brilliant reds. I was sorry when the bus began to fill up and it was time to go.

Carole made her phone call when we got back to harbor, and she told me she could get the films at six thirty, it then being four. The man with the films would meet her outside the Canadian Express office. We walked to the Empress for a drink.

The Empress is another reason for going to Victoria. It was built before people decided hotels were money-making enterprises, and takes up a couple of acres with grounds alone. The building is huge, and there are terrace rooms, nearly formal rooms, lounges off the lobbies, and a complete collection of little and big places where you can drink in decadent gentility. It reminds you of Empire and the White Man's Burden, when the sun never set on lands where the Queen's writ ran, and no matter where you were some shadow of law and maybe even justice followed. It reminds you of Cecil Rhodes and Warren Hastings, the thin red line, and the Widow of Windsor. "Walk wide of the Widow o' Windsor, for half of creation she owns," Kipling said. It may be a good idea that the old Empire is no more, but I'm sorry there's so little left of the grand tradition that built the Empress.

We had gin and tonics on the terrace, sitting in chairs that younger sons had sat in before they made the big jump to the Klondike. They had a last drink and went off to incredible adventure, and here I was, acting like I was in love with a twenty-year-old kid for my great entry into the world of counterespionage. It wasn't a favorable contrast.

I was in a blue reverie, and Carole noticed it. "What's the matter, sweetheart?" she asked.

I tried to explain it, but her whole outlook is geared against that sort of thing, so I didn't get far. It might scare her to hear me talk about deeds of derring-do and so forth. But I tried. Of course I couldn't even hint at what my real problem was.

"Paul, you're an incurable romantic, just like me. I don't think it's silly to wish there were peace and order and justice everywhere."

I didn't even try to explain that it was more than that. She looked at me again and said, "I know what's wrong with you, and I know just what to do about it. You wait right here. No, better, meet me at the boat in about an hour. I want to get something to surprise you."

"What?"

"Oh, I'm not going to tell you. You have another couple of drinks and meet me at the boat. Bye." She blew me a kiss and was off, and I sat there for a minute thinking about how nice she was. I had ordered another drink when it came to me I was supposed to be doing a job. I left my drink on the table, set down the bag of cookies we had bought from a little bakery, so the waiter would know I'd be back, and went to the men's room. Talk about sybaritic luxury, that place had enough marble to make a fair-sized courthouse all by itself. I left the men's room and turned the wrong way to reach the terrace, and ended up in a telephone booth I'd noticed when we walked around the hotel. This telephone had the advantage of being nestled in a corner so that you couldn't see into it without whoever was in it seeing you.

I called the local number Shearing had given me.

"Yes," a voice answered. It sounded vaguely Canadian.

"Larry," I answered.

"Did you have a good trip? See any whales?" he asked. It didn't sound very Canadian, but it didn't sound American either.

"No whales, but three seals swimming in a circle."

"Yes, Larry."

"She's gone off. Said she was to meet a man about getting some films of the war to smuggle into the U.S., but wasn't supposed to get them until six tonight. But she gave me a story about how she was going to get me a present for a surprise and took off. Not two minutes ago, from the Empress. She's wearing a yellow and pink afternoon dress. Flat shoes."

"Right. Just a minute." He was off the line a while, then came back on. "Anything else?"

"Nothing important. Do I carry the cargo?"

"Oh my, yes. Be sure you mark the lock papers the way we told you to when you arrive in Seattle, so we can have somebody meet you. Did you like the gardens?"

"Sure. Who was he?"

"That would be telling. You haven't spotted our man, have you?"

"No. I thought there'd been a slip. He's good. I haven't seen him."

"If it's any interest to you," he told me, "we don't think anybody is paying you any attention. All right, where are you supposed to meet her?"

"At the boat in about forty-five minutes. I have a drink warming on the terrace."

"Right. Ah, here it is now. She was followed from the Empress. You don't have to worry. Let the harbor master know when you're leaving, will you?"

"Sure. Good-bye." The connection went, and I went back to finish my drink. There was still ice in it, but the mood was gone and it didn't taste nearly as good. Hell, I'd almost let her get to me, with her off to buy me a present bit. What would make it worse would be if that's all she had done.

She had an armful of boxes when she came aboard. Four were big, flat square-shaped things, but one was about the size of a small shoebox. She set the stuff down and said, "I'm sorry, Paul, I really did go out to get you a present, but I ran into my friend with the films. He's a little worried about doing this, and he'd rather not meet you, so I brought them from his office. Can you put them somewhere?"

"Sure. Bit sneaky, aren't you?"

"Oh, please don't get mad, Paul. I know it seems like a dirty trick, but don't look like that . . ." She broke off when she saw I was laughing.

"Princess," I told her, "I don't blame your mysterious friend a bit. If I was smuggling something embarrassing I sure wouldn't want a total stranger to know it, no matter how much you might tell me about what a great fellow he was." I took the boxes, which seemed to be ordinary film mailing boxes with heavy paper around them, and stowed them under one of the berths. This particular space had a hasp and staple, and I dug out a padlock from the tool kit and snapped it on. Then I handed her the key.

"Here, kid," I told her. "It's your film, so you take it. The less I have to do with this operation the less I have to keep secret, huh? Now let's go have a good time."

I was still in the cabin. She climbed down from on deck with the other box in her hand, put it down, and pulled me to her. "Maybe you don't like me to say I love you out there on deck, but there's nothing to stop me from proving it in here, is there?" She kissed me and pulled me down on the bunk. I sat on the box she had put there. "Blast!"

"What's wrong?" she asked. "Oh, you sat on the present. Good thing it was wrapped. Look."

I tore off the paper and opened it. Inside was another box, an old leather one, with a brass catch. I opened that, and there was a short knife in a sheath. The hilt was black leather with silver embossing, and had a silver crest at the tip.

"Hey, Carole, that's beautiful. A real skean dhu. You know, we always say the same thing, but it's really *just* what I've always wanted. It's great."

"I thought that would cheer your romantic heart. Now, where were we?" She lay back on the bunk and opened her arms.

8

FOR DINNER, I had reservations at a place I'd been told
about out toward Esquimault. I forget the name, but
it's owned by a former RAF wing commander, and it's
more like being invited to dinner at his house than
eating at a restaurant. I made a big thing out of locking
the boat before we left, but I couldn't help thinking how
futile that was. I didn't know, but it was a fair guess
that the Reds had somebody watching the boat now that
those boxes were aboard. I didn't have to guess that one
of Shearing's people, and maybe the Canadian Police,
were watching. All in all, I could feel sorry for some little thief who had a bit of honest burglary in mind that
night.

The taxi took us around the harbor and sea wall on
the way, and I had the driver stop so we could walk out
to the edge where the waves rolled in. I don't know what
it was, but there's something different about that sea
wall. Maybe it's because the waves roll right down the
Straits from the Pacific, and the tide rips are strong so
that the swirls and patterns in the water are not like
anywhere else.

As I said, it was more like having dinner in the wing
commander's house than going out to a restaurant. The
house is an old Victorian mansion, the furniture is an-
tique, and you can sit in the library with a glass of sherry
while they prepare your dinner. We had roast beef and
about a ton of Yorkshire pudding, and a plum pudding
dessert, and sweetmeats with coffee, and finally brandy.
If you're ever in Victoria, look up a place out toward
Esquimault and go there. It has a replica of Shake-
speare's birthplace on the grounds, and rose gardens,
and I expect most anybody in Victoria can tell you how

to find it. It's worth asking about.

It was quite late when the taxi brought us back. Actually it was only about ten o'clock but you have the feeling that's late in Victoria. At least I did, but Carole said, "Let's go to the Empress and soak up some more of that atmosphere."

"You soak up the atmosphere," I told her. "I want a chance to soak up some more of that gin. Or maybe another brandy. Ye gods these Canadians drink well. Makes our stuff seem like swill. Remember that wine with dinner?"

We walked up to the Empress. From the hotel you can look back and see the Parliament Building all outlined in lights. It's quite a sight. Some of this may be a show for us tourists, but it's a subtle show. Not like Fort Walton Beach.

We were about halfway through our drink when Carole pointed behind me and said, "Oh look, Paul, there's Dick and Nancy!"

I looked around. It was a bit of a shock. I mean, I expected somebody, but hardly them. They'd seemed so ordinary. Hell, I hadn't even given their names to Shearing's people. Carole stood up and they came over, and we insisted they join us.

"Can't say I'm surprised," Dick said, "because we thought we might run into you people here. You gave us the idea of coming again, you know, talking about your vacation."

"Yes," Nancy put in. "We always wanted to come back, and when Carole told us she was coming with you, I bugged Dick until he said he'd bring me."

I said something about how it was nice to see them again, and Carole said something else to the same effect. The waiter was right there. That's another thing about the Empress, the waiters aren't servile, but they do act like it's a pleasure to serve you. There's an art to that.

I ordered drinks for all of us, and when the waiter left, Dick said, "That's nice of you Paul, but I better tell you we're on such a short budget this trip I can't afford to stand a round. We had just enough for one drink each in this place."

"Forget it," I told him. "I was a student myself once. Hell, I'll put the boat in at Camano and look over the development I'm supposed to be consultant on, and charge off half this trip on my income taxes. Nice to have some company."

Carole said something about the dinner we'd just had, to change the subject, and the next half hour was spent with the girls telling each other all the great things they'd done. They finally ran down, and I asked Dick; "How'd you get over? Bring your car?"

"No, I don't think it would make it that far. We came on the ferry direct from Seattle. Have to go back tomorrow."

"Oh, out of time?" I asked him.

"No, money. Just can't afford it. I'll be glad when I'm working and can be a man of leisure like you."

"Paul, I just had a thought," Carole said. "Why don't you invite Dick and Nancy to sail back with us? You said you were leaving tomorrow."

"Yeah," I said. "That's a good plan. You people have a place to stay tonight?"

They nodded. "Little hotel up the street. We came here for a drink, but . . ."

"Okay, look, you meet us here tomorrow at noon," I told them. "You cash in your return tickets for the ferry, and we'll start back in the afternoon. I want to get out of shipping lanes before dark. We can sail across to Orcas, put in at one of the San Juans for the night, and cruise around the Islands Saturday. Victoria always gets too American touristy on weekends anyway." I figured as long as I was out as bait I might as well attract everything interested. The trouble was, I still couldn't see these kids as enemy agents, any more than Carole. Hell, suppose her boxes really were films, and talk about our trip really had made Dick and Nancy decide to come up here? Suppose even that they were fishing for a free trip home. Why not? I might have done the same thing myself when I was in their situation. Oh, well, it looked like a fun trip, if a little restricted on the sex. There isn't much privacy on the *Witch*.

The weather was fine the next day, except there wasn't any wind. I dashed off a quick note for Shearing when I checked out with the harbor master, and walked out wondering if I'd bump into the mountie type who'd be along to collect it. I didn't. I had yet to see any sign of the surveillance we were supposed to be under.

We motored out of the harbor and turned east to the San Juans. The wind came up later, and by mid-afternoon there was a real blow. Dick and Nancy whooped around the deck, Carole got to take the tiller and show off for her friends, and the whole thing was fun, even when the girls dumped our dinner in the bilges halfway through cooking and had to start over. Before they did I showed them how to latch the tops of the pressure cookers.

After dark we anchored in a protected cove. A hundred feet away you could see thirty-knot winds lash up a sea against the tide, big whitecaps and foam blowing in the moonlight. Inside our cove it was calm, the trees on shore blocked off most of the wind, and in the bright light we could even see down into the water. We all sat on deck and drank Irish coffee, and laughed about the antics of a couple of current congressmen trying to get reelected.

The next day it was clear, and the wind was still blowing, but not so hard. We spent the day cruising around the Islands, working south but in no hurry to get there. At one uninhabited island we anchored and rowed ashore in the dinghy, and as the tide went out, the girls found some clams. We steamed them for dinner. After it was dark, I took turns with Carole sailing on south so that we could reach Seattle in daylight the next day. We alternated at the tiller until two or three in the morning, then found an anchorage in Admiralty Inlet a little north of Bush Point. When we went below we noted that Nancy and Dick seemed to be asleep in the double bunk, so I had to go back to my quarter berth.

With the wind and tide with you, it's not such a very

long run to Seattle from Bush. We didn't rush it, and by four we were in the locks. I filled out the lock papers completely, adding Dick and Nancy's names on the back and marked the form the special way I had been told to. We were under power in the locks, but I had left the sails up hoping for enough wind to sail down the canal. There was too much traffic, though, and the drawbridges don't always open as fast as they are supposed to, so we furled the sails and lashed them to the deck. There's always something about a sailboat with her sails furled. She looks better that way than if you take them off and stow them in their bags.

We came up to the Fremont Bridge and it opened for us, and we were in Lake Union. It always gives me a feeling of power to make the bridges open and stop traffic. Very few powerboats are big enough, of course. Once when I was being towed alongside a fifty-foot powerboat, my boat at that time being a twenty-two-foot sloop, they had to open the Fremont Bridge for me. The skipper of the powerboat told me that in ten years sailing they'd never opened it for him. He obviously enjoyed looking at the traffic piled up waiting for us to go through. It was all local traffic, because a hundred feet above is the Aurora Highway Bridge.

Dick suggested we take them directly to their houseboat, which wasn't far from the bridge. I didn't want to, but there wasn't any plausible reason why I shouldn't. I asked about the docking facilities, but they were adequate, and the fact was that as they lived just across the lake from where I kept *Witch*, it was much shorter getting them home by water than by land. They lived in a complex of houseboats off Western Avenue. These weren't like the ones where the student party had been. The Western Avenue houseboats are mostly owned by the people living in them, and are painted and kept up. They even have a community-maintained raft, with dirt piled on it, that they grow flowers on. There is also a landing float where Dick and Nancy got off. I took a quick check to see that the film boxes were still in their locker, while Carole helped them get their luggage ashore. Carole must have taken the paper off while I was rowing people around in the dinghy, because brown plastic boxes with metal corner reinforcements were now in the locker. The boxes were closed with straps.

Carole and I motored back to our berth and tied *Witch* up. "The devil with it hon," I said. "Let's just get the boat secure and go home. I can clean her up in a couple of days. Right now I want a shower and a little rest."

She agreed. We'd had a good time, but we were both beat. I got our wet things and dirty clothes out, and Carole packed her films in a laundry bag. We left everything else.

It was twilight when we reached home. I unlocked the door, and we went in through the hall and kitchen to the dining room, which functions as a kind of central room to my house. I dumped what I was carrying on the floor and started to stretch, when men came out of the bedroom and living room. Louis Alessandro was the last one in.

Alessandro didn't say anything. There was a uniformed Seattle policeman, three plainclothesmen, and Alessandro. One of the plainclothesmen held out a Treasury badge and said, "Paul Crane and Carole Halleck, I have here a warrant for your arrests and a search warrant for these premises and your personal effects. I must warn you that anything you say may be taken in evidence against you, and you have a right to remain silent."

Carole gasped and clutched the laundry bag tighter. Alessandro didn't act like he'd ever seen me before. I had had no warning of this, and didn't have the remotest idea of what I should do, but it seemed that maintaining my cover would be a good idea. I looked at the Treasury agent and said, "May I ask what the charge is?"

"Oh, we have several of them," he said. "Suspicion of smuggling, suspicion of violation of state and federal narcotics laws, you name it. May I see what's in those bags you brought in?"

There wasn't any point in making a scene, but Carole tried to hold on to her laundry bag. The uniformed cop took it.

"Narcotics," Carole said. "What in the world are you talking about?" As the officer fished out the film boxes, she said, "Since when is it a crime to bring films home with you from a trip?"

"Do you acknowledge ownership of these boxes?" the T-man asked her.

"Don't answer him, Carole," I said. He turned to me and said, "Okay, buddy, either you keep quiet or we separate you. Have it your way, but the next thing you say like that, I'll take you in the other room."

Carole didn't pay any attention anyway. "Yes, they're mine," she told them. "Paul had nothing to do with bringing them here. He didn't even know about them. Sure I brought some films into the country. We're supposed to have freedom of speech in this country, and look what happens when we bring in some pictures of what our airplanes are doing over there. Freedom of speech, yet. Five strong men to take some films away from one girl."

One of the plainclothes guys and the harness bull opened the straps of the film cans. They got the straps open on each one before they took the lid off the first box. In the box was a round film can, sealed with tape. They had to tear the tape, which was some kind of plastic stuff, to open the can. Inside the can was an ordinary spool of film.

Each box was opened in turn, and inside was the same can, and after the tape was torn off the can, there was nothing in it but a spool of film, except that the thicker box had two spools of film. There wasn't a sign of anything else.

"God damn it," Alessandro exploded. He charged over and stood right in front of me, his fists clenched, and yelled in my face, "Where's the stuff, you son of a bitch."

It came to me this had to be an act. I've heard the training they put FBI men through, and I never heard of one losing his cool like this. But if it was an act, it was damn convincing. I still wasn't sure he wouldn't push my teeth in. We were about the same size, but I hadn't any doubt that with his training he could take me apart.

"What stuff?" I asked as innocently as I knew how. He actually clenched his fist. "Hold it, Louis," the Treasury guy said. Alessandro stood there glaring at me and the T-man looked over at Carole and said, "You admit that this material is yours, and that you brought it into the country undeclared and uninspected, acting without the knowledge of the captain of the vessel on which you were traveling?"

Carole nodded. The T-guy didn't think that was good enough, and asked his question again.

"Yes," she shouted. "Yes, yes, yes! Paul didn't know about it. I put it on the boat when he was ashore. It's all mine and you can't accuse him of anything."

I started to say something. She was being noble as hell about it, and I felt like a worm. I didn't though. If she and the government people were both trying to accomplish the same thing, why should I interfere? There had to be more to it than that.

"All right," the Treasury agent said. "Take her downtown. We can hold her on the smuggling charge anyway."

The plainclothesman who hadn't said anything took out handcuffs and clipped them to Carole and then himself. Then I looked at him again. He was wearing a coat just like the topcoat I was carrying over my arm when I came into the house, and he had on my hat out of my closet. He was my height, and in the dark it would be very easy to mistake him for me. Anybody seeing him handcuffed to Carole in the near dark outside would believe they had arrested both of us, if they played it right, and it was too much to be a coincidence. It figured that they would make it look like I was going downtown too. The other plainclothesman and the uniformed policeman took them out, the uniform leading the way. The boss T-man brought up the rear. When we heard the outside door close, Harry Shearing came out of my bedroom.

Alessandro still looked mad as hell. "Where is the stuff, damn it?" he demanded.

I told them about Dick and Nancy, gave their descriptions, and described the houseboat complex they lived in. I didn't know the address of the houseboat, but I had watched them until they went into one, so I could say which one it was. Alessandro rushed off to the phone, but Shearing just poured some coffee, handed me a cup, and poured himself some.

"The place is clean, Paul. We went over it ourselves. So we can talk. You've done some good work."

I started to answer, but there was an explosion outside. I ran for the window, but before I could get there, Shearing grabbed me and threw me into a chair. He hadn't seemed to use any particular effort to do it, but I found myself sitting down. "Don't be stupid," he said. He was quite calm. "Stay there and stay away from windows. I don't want you seen." Then he broke and ran for the front door. Alessandro had dropped the telephone and was out just in front of him.

I sat there for a minute, but it wasn't easy. I could hear people running and shouting outside, and cars stopping in the street. Finally I couldn't take anymore and went to the hall. They had left the front door open, but it was closed far enough that you couldn't see the stairs from outside. I went up the stairs on my knees so I couldn't be seen through the stair window, and went into the upstairs front bedroom I didn't use anymore. It had lacy curtains, and with the door closed and the lights off nobody could see me when I looked out. The only trouble was I couldn't see a thing. There were several cars stopped in front of the house, and people were running toward a spot down the street past where I could see. That didn't tell me any more than I knew before, so I made it back down the stairs and sat where Shearing had pitched me. It seemed to take forever before I heard a siren, then another. Finally Shearing and Alessandro came back in alone.

"What in God's name happened?" I asked.

Alessandro was cursing under his breath. He turned to Shearing and said, "You and your goddamned clever plans. One of my men, one of yours, a Treasury agent, and a cop. Not to mention the girl. And the stuff's loose in the city. That's it, Shearing. That's the end of it." He put the telephone receiver, which I had forgotten, back on the hook, then picked it up and dialed a number.

I shouted at Shearing, "What in hell is going on?" but he didn't say anything. Alessandro got his number and said, "Alessandro here. Give me Prescott." It didn't take a moment. "Prescott? Run it. The whole thing. I want every damn pusher and agent rounded up. Get started organizing the city and county people, I'll be right down." He hung up, glared at Shearing, and when nobody said anything, went out. We heard the door slam.

As calmly as I could, I said, "Will you please tell me what is happening? What was that noise? What did he mean, 'Not to mention the girl'?"

"You were beginning to fall for that kid, weren't you? She's dead, Crane. They're all dead. The cop, Benson, Carruthers, Louis' man, and the girl. Somebody put a hand grenade in the car just as they were closing the doors."

"Good God, what for? Who?"

"One of the dope gang. A hophead. Louis got him just as he grabbed the film cans and started to run. They took him downtown, but they won't get anything out of him. He won't know anything, except maybe about the dope operation and who sent him, and they won't get that out of him either. We might, but now that he's under arrest by the regulars he'll never talk. With luck he'll get life, which means about seven years in this state, the way the courts have been handling it."

I sat down. It was hard to realize that she was dead. I still didn't believe she was anything more than it looked like, a kid who got too involved with saving the world. They'd let her carry the mail and then killed her. Shearing was still talking.

"We thought they might have somebody watching this place," he was saying, "and Louis and the Treasury people insisted that the heroin had to be seized as soon as it got here. I persuaded them to let you off. Seemed like a good idea at the time, because if you were in custody I couldn't talk to you without letting the connection get out to too many people. I still can't figure out why they did this. They must have sent a prime case to watch your place, and when he saw all that stuff being taken downtown he pulled this. That would mean at least some of them don't know Wahlke took the junk off with him. Have you got anything to drink?"

I didn't really hear him, but some part of me did and got up. I took out a bottle of Scotch and poured each of us a big slug. Shearing drained his off and said, "At least, I think that's it. If the guy wasn't after the junk, it means they thought the kid knew too much and might have spilled some to you, so they wanted you both out of the way. Damn it, I don't even know which of you they wanted, if they wanted either of you. The kid stuck up for you."

"Yeah, she did, and I let her, and I let them take her out to that car . . ."

"What in hell do you mean, you let them take her?" Shearing demanded. "Get off the martyr crap and talk sense. You didn't have a damn bit of control over what happened here. Turned out neither did we, but you sure as hell didn't. Now are you going to sit there and drink Scotch and feel sorry for yourself, or are you going to help me get this job done? We've still got work to do, and if you're interested in doing something about the people who killed the girl you'll help. Let's get on with it."

"Work? How? You mean catching Nancy and Dick? I told you all I know about them. I still don't know why Alessandro was so surprised. I marked the lock papers the way you told me to."

"Sure you did," Shearing said. "But Louis never got the message because I never passed it on. He'd want to arrest them. You have to remember, the Treasury people are only interested in stopping the flow of narcotics. The FBI has a counterespionage mission, but they have to play by the rules, and when the Treasury and Secret Service boys yell loud enough Louis has to roll over and play dead. You don't need to worry about Wahlke. I had a man at Western when you let them off, and I'll find out who Wahlke hands the stuff to. He'd probably want to get rid of it before you even got to shore, so my people ought to know something right now. Our problem now is that Louis won't wait to pull off this big cleanup campaign of his. He'll organize the roundup when he gets back to his office, so we don't have much time to try to connect the dope people to the Chicom agents. Much as I like Louis, why the hell couldn't he have been in that car instead of Carruthers?''

It was still hard for me to think. I kept remembering Carole, and I kept expecting her to come in the door. Her jacket was lying there in the middle of the dining room, and I took it in and hung it up with some of her other things in my closet.

I poured myself another shot of Scotch, and told Shearing, "You know, I still don't know that there was anything in those packages but film. I wonder if they weigh any different from when I handled them in Victoria?''

"There was something. That guy wouldn't have tossed a grenade over some war pictures. Come on, use your head. I know you're shook up, but we have things to do. Look here.''

He had a whole sheaf of photographs. As he handed them to me he said, "The Mountie in Victoria took them. Everybody in the terminal when she got the stuff. Your chick got the films out of a dead drop, but sometimes these guys like to be clever and watch the pickup. A real pro wouldn't, but there's nothing that says pro about this operation so far. See if you recognize anybody.

The pictures were of the ferry dock in Victoria. There were several dozen, all obviously unposed, and as I went through them I began to think I recognized half the faces, but of course I didn't. Then one stood out.

"Roger Balsinger?'' I said. I mean it was a real shock.

"You know him? Who is he? You never mentioned any Balsingers that I can remember."

I told him about Roger and where I'd seen him last.

"I wonder about you, Crane. I really do." Shearing shook his head and made a face. "Here a guy practically pushes the chick into your boat for the trip and you don't think it's worth reporting. Jeez, if they'd just give me a decent operation so I didn't have to use all those amateurs." He took another drink. "Sorry, Paul, I don't really mean that. You've done a pretty good job all told. Hell, a damn good job." He picked up the telephone and dialed the headquarters number. "Shearing. Yeah, the lost sheep got found, and I'll see you next Groundhog Day. I think we've got him. Balsinger, Roger Balsinger. Playboy type. Six-two, about 180, sandy brown hair, cut short. Dresses in conservative suits or sports coat and tie. Drives a TR4, silver. Address 5348 University Way, an apartment there, number unknown. Hangs around the University District a lot. Frequents coffeehouses, taverns. Works in an insurance brokerage house, may have his name in the firm title. Family lives out near Sand Point somewhere—yeah, it's those Balsingers. They're presumably not involved. I want this guy. I want him alive, and I don't want anyone else to know we've got him. The Friendly Neighbors are starting their drive—yeah, okay, so you got the word. We need this Balsinger type before then if we can get him. We want any papers he might have, anything at all. I'm proceeding to his apartment now. Send an expert; I want that place taken apart. Yeah, I'm that sure. He's got to be it. May be a big one. Okay, go at it." Shearing hung up. "Paul, you've earned your way into it if you want. Want to come with me? Might make it easier for me to get in that place if he's home."

"Sure, but I can't see Roger as a master spy. He's a clod. And what in hell would he do it for? The only thing he likes is himself. He sure wouldn't be loyal to anything."

"How should I know?" Shearing remarked. It seemed a reasonable statement. "We do know he was in Victoria—right where the stuff was handed over—

which makes him the cut-out man between whoever furnished the stuff and the delivery agent. He's valuable enough to get out of carrying the mail when they're desperate for it. He shows up to look you over and gives the chick the word that she's to go. He associates with money and his family's rich so he can handle good-sized amounts without anything special being thought of it. If we're wrong we'll apologize, but I don't think we are. Do you?''

9

WHILE SHEARING WATCHED, I got out the little five-shot .38 Chief's Special they'd given me and clipped its holster on my belt. I put some extra cartridges in my pocket, and pulled on a trenchcoat I hadn't worn for years. It would look a little conspicuous, because even in the rain in Seattle we generally don't wear raincoats, but it might keep anybody from recognizing me when we went out. I also pulled on a hat, and we went out the back way. I left the Barracuda sitting in front of the curb and we took Shearing's Impala.

It isn't far from my place to the apartment where Roger lived. Shearing seemed to know his way around the District, cutting through residential streets rather than going up University Way where there are people and traffic lights. We went in the back way and through the hall to the mailboxes. Roger lived on the second floor. This was a nice apartment building, a new one, but designed with inside halls and outside balconies for the apartments. It kept people from seeing who was visiting you unless they opened their doors, and I wondered if that was why Roger had chosen it.

Nobody answered the bell. Shearing took out a little plastic ribbon and tried it on the door, but nothing happened. He put it back in his pocket and looked at the door again. "That's interesting," he said. "Any other door in the building I could open with this, but he's done things to his lock." He took out a flat leather tool roll from his coat pocket. I hadn't noticed it before, so he must have brought it from the car. It still took him about five minutes, with me worrying that somebody would see us and call the police, but finally there was a splintering sound and the door opened. Shearing had his pistol out as he went in. A little self-consciously, I drew mine. There wasn't any need for it. Nobody was in the place.

"Let's see what we have here," Shearing said after he closed the door. "You watch the door. If he comes in, let him. Say something nice to him. Get him inside and we'll take him." I sat down facing the door but off to the side where you wouldn't be able to see me immediately if you came in, and Shearing began to go through the place.

He was very systematic. He started with the desk, and looked at every paper, book and object in or on it. As he finished with each item he put it in one of three piles he was making. I noticed that one pile had all the books he found, which presumably meant they would be examined again for codes or something. When he finished with the loose objects, he took drawers out of the desk and looked at both sides, measured their depth inside and outside, and looked into the holes they had come out of.

He was about finished with the desk when there was a knock at the door. Shearing stood against the wall on one side, and I moved to the other. The bell rang, then there was another knock. Then the door opened, and a man about my size came in. Shearing relaxed.

"George, this is Paul. George is on our side. Okay, Paul, you go back to watching. You got somebody outside?" he asked George.

"Janie. There's nobody else," he went on when Shearing gave him a funny look. "I've got to keep liaison with the Neighbors, and I've got everybody else either tailing Wahlke and Snow to see what they do with the stuff, or out looking for your chum Balsinger. Incidentally, Wahlke's got the junk on him, or it looks good anyway. He's carrying a little briefcase around and I can't think why, the places he's going. May be distributing. Got some names and addresses for you."

"Good. Now let's take this place apart," Shearing told him. George went in the other room. They searched for over an hour and Roger's nice playboy apartment would never be the same when they finished with it. They tore furniture apart, slashed the linings out of luggage, took any solid object they could apart, and generally wrecked the place. Then George called from the bedroom, "Here's something." He came in with a little cheap black-bound financial journal such as they sell in dime stores. "Inside the headboard of his bed. Neat little box in there, would have missed it if we weren't taking the place apart."

They looked at it, and I watched over their shoulders. It had mostly strings of numbers, with a few words that didn't seem to mean anything. I couldn't make any sense out of it, but they didn't seem to be able to either.

"Must be a pretty simple code," Shearing said. "He wouldn't have it if it didn't mean something to him, and nobody can keep that much in his head. Unless he's got a computer."

"Hey," I said. "What about his insurance office? It might have an office computer. If it's a simple code, he might be able to use that, those office machines don't have a big memory capacity but they will handle a lot of bookkeeping."

"Good thinking," George told me. "I'll check it out, shall I?"

"Later," Shearing told him. "Right now I want Balsinger. You stay here and keep watch on this place. See what else you can find. I'm taking Janie off the outside, so be careful. Let's go, Paul."

On the way out, Shearing used some of Roger's Old English Scratch Remover furniture polish to hide the damage to the door. When he finished, you'd have to look close to see that it had been forced, and they fixed the lock so that it would work again. George stayed inside and we went down the stairs and out.

Outside, the mist made halos around each street light. Shearing signaled with his arm, and a couple of minutes later Janie joined us in his car. We turned the lights out and sat watching the apartment building while we talked. Shearing tuned in a station on the radio and we waited for the news.

"How much did George tell you?" Shearing asked Janie.

"Most of it, I guess. The grenade business, Balsinger, and Alessandro's orders. Is there anything else?"

"No," he said. "We've got maybe until dawn before the word gets out about the roundup. Louis will do it right and try to get everybody he can at one time, and he's got sense enough to keep anybody who knows about it away from a telephone." I remembered that I hadn't been out of sight after I heard Alessandro's instructions, and wondered if he meant that for me.

"What do we do, just wait?" I asked. "There must be something better we can do. Why don't you want anybody to see me?"

"Because you may be officially dead, and while I don't right now know how I can use that I don't throw anything away for nothing. Listen," Shearing said.

The record droned off and we were spared further laments about the teenage girl watching from the sky. A newscaster came on. "The latest word about the explosion in the University District seems to be that there was a definite attack on a police car. Black Power literature was found scattered at the scene, and police have refused to answer any questions put by reporters. One reporter has announced that eyewitnesses saw a Negro apprehended at the scene of the explosion, but police refuse to comment on that as well.

"There were at least four persons killed in the explosion, which seems to have been caused by a hand grenade. At least two were police officers, and there is speculation that the other two, one of whom was a woman, were prisoners under arrest. Police are withholding the names of the victims pending notification of next of kin.

"Speculation further has it that the police had arrested two members of the anti-war committee of the university and were about to take them to police headquarters when the car was attacked. It is not known whether the attack was related to the arrests or was a separate incident. For further bulletins, stay tuned to this station. Next regular news at eleven o'clock."

Janie switched off the radio. "We know Balsinger's in this. Is there anyone else we can try to pick up before Louis' dragnet gets them?"

"I don't know," Shearing answered her. "George found what may be a record book. If it is, and we can decode it in time, there might be. I'm going to run it down to headquarters and roust up what talent I can find. What do you think you and Crane could do before morning?"

"Well," she said, "we could go look for Balsinger around the District. Paul could take me to the places he might go."

"What do you think Paul? I can't see any real reason for reporting you dead. Nobody knows the Halleck girl is dead either, except whoever sent the hophead to watch your place. They won't know about you and where you fit in, and somebody might take an interest tonight. By tomorrow there won't be anything to do but round up the pieces, if Louis leaves any. If we don't get Balsinger, or crack this code, I doubt we'll get any top people and I'll be back where I started. They'll still have money, Balsinger will go to ground, and I won't have a lead on the espionage net."

"Won't you be compromising Janie?" I asked.

"They know I'm connected with you one way or another, we made that obvious," she said. "If they know which side you're on, they'll know about me as well. If they don't, being seen with you won't hurt anyway."

"Yeah, that's all great," I told them, "but what in hell do I say about Carole? It may not seem funny to you characters that a girl goes off on a weekend trip with a guy and turns up dead, but normal people might sense a connection. I for one would wonder what in hell Paul Crane was doing walking the streets with another girl when his chick had just been splattered all over the landscape in front of his house." They were so damn calm, and I wanted to scream.

Shearing shook his head. "It wasn't in front of your house, it was in the middle of the next block. You lie, is what you do. You tell them Carole brought back some films and took them out to give somebody, and you haven't seen her since. You tell them you weren't home when the bang happened. You act a little worried about her, but not too much because you had a fight with her on the way back. Hell, you use your judgment. If you don't like that, you could try going fishing and get out of the way while we try to get something out of this fouled up mess.''

"You cold-blooded son of a bitch," I told him. It was getting to me. "I know what I can do. I can go out and try to find out who gave a moron with a grenade and a fistful of Black Power literature the job of watching my house. Those bastards were laying for Carole and me, and if you aren't interested in who wanted that done, I am." I opened the door of the car and got out. I thought Shearing might try to stop me, but all he did was nod at Janie. She got out too, and Shearing drove away, fast.

"What in hell do you think you're doing?" I asked her.

"I'm staying with you to make sure you don't warn anybody about Louis Alessandro's show tomorrow morning. And incidentally to have somebody available to vouch for me, too. You don't think he'd leave either one of us alone tonight, do you?"

"What's to keep me from running out on you, doll? You can't keep up with me."

"Nothing, Paul. But you'd be in a hell of a mess if somebody does let it leak and you had left me, wouldn't you?"

I started to walk to my house, but remembering that she didn't like to walk fast, I kept the pace down. I couldn't help remembering a girl who could keep up with me.

I was trying to think. All I had done up to now was let other people tell me what to do. It had been a game. Hell, it all started as a game, going out to play policeman with Danny. Then play spy with Carole. I wasn't worked up over Danny any more, I'd shot his killer myself, even if it was more of an accident than revenge, but I wanted more than an accident for the bastard who had Carole killed. I wanted his neck in my hands. It seemed to me maybe there would be a few other people who didn't like being used.

I didn't say anything to Janie when I got to my car, just unlocked the door for her and got in on the other side. While I warmed it up, she said, "I know you don't feel like talking, but where are you going?"

"You'll see. I'm not going off to warn anybody, if that's what you mean."

I just about blew it by driving too fast. My little Formula S Barracuda may not be a sports car, but she'll do better than most buggies you drive on streets. At least she will for me. I can't do a lot of spectacular things, but I can drive cars. There was a time when I drove in sports car races down at Shelton, and while that might have been a while ago, you don't forget how. It's a miracle we didn't get a ticket.

Sunday nights are quiet in Seattle. Sometimes there are parties, but not too often, and most of the coffeehouses close early. You can find people at home, alone, on Sunday nights. I was hoping I could, anyway.

I drove to Ron's houseboat. We walked up the gangways past the other houseboats, and nothing moved except some of the alley cats who seem to live around the boats but never belong to anybody. There was a light in Ron's place, and he opened the door right away. I couldn't see anybody else around.

He was drunk. This was one weekend he hadn't forgotten to stock up.

"H'lo, Paul. Come in. Who's your new chick?"

"She's not my chick, she's my watchdog. Do you know Carole's dead?"

He didn't say anything. I've known Ron for years. He's a drunk, and maybe there's a lot wrong with him, but he's a lousy liar and always has been, and I could tell. He hadn't known. It was a real shock to him.

"She's dead. Somebody arranged for her to bring something into the country from Canada, and then he sent one of his friends with a hand grenade to make sure she didn't talk about it. One of your friends, Ron. One of the antiwar group. She thought she was carrying antiwar films, so it had to be one of that gang.''

"Hey, no, man! You're putting me on," he said. He sat down on the cheap flowered rug and drained the glass he'd left there when he answered the door. "You gotta be putting me on. Who'd do that?''

"You tell me who'd do that. You tell me who'd use her to do his dirty work and then kill her. You know what else he did? He didn't waste her dying, either. He had her killed so it would look like a Black Power plot, so he could use that to get a little race hate going. Now you tell me who'd like a race riot. Who's the big true believer, Ron? Who'd do anything for the cause?''

He put his hands to his head and squeezed hard, shaking his head in his hands. He got the bottle of whiskey and tried to pour a drink, but his hands shook and he didn't get much in the glass. Finally he drank it out of the bottle. I just looked at him.

He looked up at me and said, "How would I know. Hey, hey, no man, you don't think I'd do that. You don't think me.''

"No," I told him. "I don't think you. But I think somebody's been asking around about me lately. I think somebody's talked to you about Carole, and could they trust her to do something for the movement. I think somebody's shown a lot of interest in our trip, and you damn well know who it was. Now goddamn it, Ron, I want to know. I'm going to kill the bastard and you're going to tell me who it is.''

It was pitiful to watch him. Everything he'd lived for was coming apart, and you could see it happening to him. His causes, peace, brotherhood, and all the rest of it, and it ended up with a girl dead. A girl he'd liked. He wanted to believe I was a liar, but he knew better. He knew I wasn't acting because I wasn't, and he'd known for a long time there were people in his organizations who'd do something like that, but he'd never admitted it to himself.

He started to take another drink, and I slapped the glass out of his hand. Then he tried to get up and I kicked him in the crotch, not too hard, but hard enough to hurt. He fell down and whimpered.

"Who was it, Ron? You're going to tell me, the only question is whether I have to ruin you before you do. Think about it, Ron old buddy, no more girls. And when it happens, it's pain, Ron, it's pain." I kicked him again, harder than the first time, just to let him know I meant it.

He screamed this time, loud enough to disturb people outside if they were the kind of people who got disturbed.

"That won't help you," I told him. "Your buddies have passed out. Nobody gets involved here anyway, right? Everybody's cool here. Maybe when we leave somebody'll come over and ask you what happened, if he's sober enough to get here. But it'll be too late for you. No more girls, Ron. Okay, get set, here it comes." I stepped closer to him.

"No, oh Jesus, no, don't," he moaned. "It was John Murray. He sent her for the films. She met him here one night, and he told her to go with you and bring the films back. He told her where to get them and who to call, a B.C. YPSAL member. O God, no, leave me alone."

"Where can I find him?"

"Ivar's place. Ivar's out of town, John Murray's staying there." He started shaking all over, and got hold of his bottle. I let him take a big slug, then tilted his face up so I could see it.

"Did you know about the grenade?" I asked him.

"No man, you know better. No."

He wasn't lying. He drank some more, and I hustled Janie out. Ron had done the only thing the movement could never excuse. He'd finked. If there's any honor in that crowd, it's centered around never finking on anybody. I felt a little sorry for him, but not much.

It was misting up more outside, and that made it hard to see. If anybody heard our conversation with Ron, they didn't come out to talk about it, which was probably as well for them, the way I felt. Janie hadn't said a word while we were inside, but on the way to the car she said, "Hadn't we better do something about him?"

"Short of killing him, what?" I asked her. "He used to be a friend. You kill him if you want him dead. Anyway, he's busy doing something about himself right now. I doubt he'll talk to anybody before morning." The way I said it, she didn't argue.

I was more careful driving back to the District. Now that I knew what I had to do, I wanted to be sure I got the chance. Ivar lived in a rundown old shack of a place which used to be a garage. It's not far from the ship canal, down toward the Fremont district west of the university, just outside the area students will live in. It's just too far to walk if you're late for a class, so the rents are low. Lots of the fringe crowd live around there now the university has got so big that rents have gone out of sight in the District. I can remember getting a two-room and bath apartment only four blocks from the campus for $25.00 a month. Now the same place goes for fifty and it hasn't been repaired or even cleaned since I lived there.

Janie made me stop on the way and she telephoned in the information about Murray. I didn't want to let her, but she was right, and she kept at it until I agreed. She received an okay from downtown to pick him up. They wanted to talk to him.

As we drove to Ivar's place, Janie said, "That order was to pick him up, not kill him. The mood you're in, I don't know if it's a good idea for me to let you near him."

I didn't answer for a while, then said, "You aren't letting me, and there's only one way you can stop me. Maybe I'll get him alive and maybe not. He's an ex-paratrooper, he can outshoot me, and I expect he can take me apart unarmed. I'll use whatever advantage I have. What happens if we do get him alive?"

"They question him to find out who he works for. If he's been in the San Francisco office, he may have some important information."

"He wouldn't tell you a damn thing," I told her. "John Murray's a different breed of cat from these losers. I wasn't surprised when Ron said it had to be him, I couldn't think who else was that tough."

Janie shrugged. "They usually do talk to Shearing's experts. I think they use lie detectors and things. You can get a yes-no answer from anybody with a polygraph if there's a good enough operator on it. Then you just have to ask the right questions. They have other techniques as well."

"Yeah. What happens to them after that? I mean, I never heard anybody tell a story about how he was questioned forcibly by the counterspies."

She lit a cigarette and held the match so I could see her face when she answered. "I don't know what happens to them. I never asked." She blew out the match.

I pulled up about a block from the shack. To get to it, you have to go down an alley unless you want to try climbing fences and cutting through respectable people's yards. Not too many people knew anybody lived in the alley, and there had never been a party with more than three or four at a time there. I knew about it because I had played poker a couple of times, with Ivar and some fish. Ivar was pretty good at the game and played about every week.

There was a light in the shack. The window shades were down, and since I'd been inside, I knew Ivar had taped them down to keep anybody from looking in. He was a nut on privacy. Ivar is an old guy, over fifty, and I'm told he was once some kind of officer in the IWW or something like that thirty years ago, and that's why he's still so suspicious of police. He threw Dan Ackerman out of a poker game when he found out Danny was a reserve police officer.

We got closer, and I could hear people talking, but I couldn't tell how many. I told Janie to wait outside for me, and took the little .38 out of its holster and held it in my hand in my trench-coat pocket. Then I tried the door with my left hand. It was locked, but that place is half rotten. I put my shoulder against the door and shoved, and part of the jamb tore loose.

John Murray was sitting behind the old kitchen table Ivar uses for a desk. There was a big guy standing against the wall near him, and they were looking at a city map on the table. Murray looked up, recognized me, and it looked like he'd seen a ghost.

"What's the matter, John? Think I was dead?" I asked him. "Why'd you think that? You son of a bitch, you have two choices. You can come with me, or I'll beat your brains in with my bare hands." I was leaning against what was left of the door, both hands in my pockets, and I tried to look unarmed. I wanted to see what they'd do.

"See if he's alone, Ben," Murray told the big guy. I looked at him, and I remembered seeing him before, but I'd never met him. One of the new guys, probably came up with Murray. He was taller than I am, maybe an inch or so, but he outweighed me a hundred pounds. He would have looked all right on a pro football team.

"Sure, John," Ben said. "Move, punk." He started toward me and I took the pistol out of my pocket and held it about two feet from his chest and pulled the trigger twice. The gun was loaded with wadcutters, which are good target ammunition. They are also good people ammunition because they flatten out if they hit something hard like bone, and transfer most of their energy to whatever they hit. Ben was stopped by the first slug and thrown backward by the second. He stayed on his feet for maybe a couple of seconds, but he was gone.

Murray was reaching for something. I took a step closer to him, put the gun next to his leg, and shot him in the thigh. He screamed and threw his hands to where he'd been hit, and I looked in the drawer of the table. There was a little gun in it, one of those modern high-powered .22 replicas of a Derringer pistol. I never thought they were much use, but you can carry one in a pocket.

Janie came in carrying a .38 like mine. She looked at the situation, handed the piece to me, and looked at where I'd shot Murray. As I took the gun from her I wondered where she'd kept it. Somewhere under her skirt, I figured, because there sure hadn't been any room for it anywhere else.

She found a necktie hanging in the closet and made a tourniquet around Murray's leg. "Help me get him out of here, you idiot. The neighbors will have the police here any minute."

I doubted that, because in that district kids shoot at street lights, and trucks backfire, and people mind their own business. Still, somebody might be new around there, and I didn't particularly want to explain things. I took a quick look, but as I figured, there wasn't any point in trying to carry Ben, even if I could have lifted his 270 pounds.

Murray didn't want to come. I put my gun against his ribs and said, "That's right, fat boy. Make trouble for us. I wish you would, it wasn't my idea for you to come out of this alive." He looked at me and tried to get up.

With Janie carrying her artillery again and mine tucked in its holster, I let Murray lean on me. He didn't walk too well, but he managed to hobble out and down the alley to the car. Janie looked competent enough, so I let her sit in back, with Murray next to me in the other bucket seat. Then I strapped him in with the safety belt and used his shoelace to tie his hands together in front of him.

"Where to, doll?" I asked her.

"To a telephone." She was on the phone a minute, then came back and got in the car.

"Head out toward Bothell," she said.

Driving along, I waited for the reaction. The first time I'd been involved in killing somebody, I thought I'd never get over being sick. Now all I had was a tight feeling in my stomach, and that was more worry about being stopped by the police than anything else. In fact, I was surprised to notice, I felt pretty good. I didn't miss Ben at all. If anybody looked sick, it was John Murray, although I wondered about Janie too. She didn't talk much, but then there wasn't much to say.

I got us out of the district and onto Bothell Way.

There wasn't a bit of traffic. Janie told me to go out
almost to Bothell, but I said, "That's up to Johnnie
boy. I can go to a place where they'll take care of you,
Murray, or I can take you to Samammish Slough and
turn you loose. Well, maybe not quite loose, but you'll
be found in the morning. When they find you, they'll
loosen the tourniquet, but of course gangrene will have
started by then. You'll be interested in whether taking
your leg off will stop it, won't you?" I made this as
casual as I could.

He didn't answer, but Janie piped up. "You can't do
that."

"The hell I can't, doll. I didn't agree to bring this
chump in alive for nothing. What good is he to us if he
won't talk to us? Won't be long before we get to the
Samammish turnoff," I observed.

Janie didn't say anything else, and when we got to the
turnoff I took a right, heading away from the Bothell
highway.

"Save it," Murray spat out. "You can't let the police
find me alive and we both know it. Hell, you're scared
of the police yourself."

"Are we?" I asked Janie. She shook her head. "See,
John? Ever hear of alibis? Think Janie and I can't have
the world's best by tomorrow morning? You know how
it's done. But you go on thinking I won't leave you. I'm
going to tell you one thing, baby. When I dump you off,
I'm not coming back. So you don't have very long
before you can stop worrying about what to do."

He looked at me, swiveled around to look at Janie,
then looked back at me. "She told me you went for her.
Bad. You crazy bastard, you'd do it. Just for that girl,
you'd do it. Gangrene. You never saw gangrene, did
you? You never saw a man rot to death."

"Nope. Maybe you can tell me about it. I can think
about how you'll feel for the next couple of days."

He looked at Janie, saw she wouldn't do it, but she
wouldn't stop me either. Then he looked back at me. He
was trying to figure out whether I'd really leave him out
there tied up. Well, as a matter of fact, so was I. He
decided before I did.

"All right. What do you want? Names?"

"I'll take some names," I said. "But mostly I'm interested in why you had Carole killed. Give us a name for a start."

"Roger Balsinger."

"I knew that one, but it'll do for a minute. Oh yeah, we knew it. He made one mistake too many and got tagged. Now tell me a story about Carole." I stopped the car, but I didn't make any move to turn it around, just got a plastic raincoat out from under the seat and held it under his leg while I loosened the tourniquet. He bled all over the place, in a flood, not spurts. Venous bleeding.

Janie said, "You've got to get him to a doctor before he bleeds to death. Get back on Bothell Way, it's not far from there."

I turned on the ignition and kicked over the motor, but I left her out of gear. "I'll start when he starts," I said.

"I knew you were an agent for somebody," Murray said. "The others didn't think so, and I got overruled by that Balsinger. Carole was sure you weren't working for anybody, but she was hot for you anyway. So I had to finish you before you turned up something important. The kid heard me planning it, and she got scared. Said she'd turn us all in first. I talked her out of that by making her think she didn't understand what she'd heard, but then both of you had to go. So we waited for you with the grenade. Wasn't sure of getting you at the boat, so we waited at your house."

"Why wait?" I asked him. I got the car going toward the highway.

"We needed that junk. Balsinger decided to let you bring it in. It looked to me like they might let you get in the country with it and try to see who you delivered it to. The grenade would have stopped them finding anything out anyway. Uh. Oh man, that's bad. You got anything to drink in here?"

I shook my head. "Where did Dick Wahlke and his girl, Nancy Snow, fit in?"

"Since I was on to you even if I couldn't get anybody

else to believe it, I put Wahlke on to get the junk out.
Then all you'd have was the films. What with them and
the Black Power literature, nobody would ever figure
out who wanted you out of the way. No junk, no agent,
no nothing. But we saw the cops go into your place
while we were waiting for you. Then you came screaming up in that car and got inside before we could do
anything. Too many in there to go in after you. Figured
to get you, cops and all, when you came out. Grab the
films, leave you dead with the cops and the literature
around. Cops go looking for Negroes, maybe they'd
shoot one, really get some action. I thought you were in
that car. I thought so until I saw you back there. How in
hell are you alive? You weren't in that car, everybody
in it was croaked."

"No, I wasn't in it. What about Wahlke and the girl?
How'd you think they'd get clean away?"

"How would anybody know they had anything to do
with it? The girl's clean anyway. She thinks she's
delivering LSD. Dick Wahlke's never been near us for
years. No reason for anybody to think anything about
them. No way for you to tell anybody about them until
it was too late. He's got rid of the stuff now. You
couldn't even prove a damn thing on him." He looked
worse, so I put on some speed. We got to the highway
and turned out toward Bothell. His voice was becoming
weaker all the time.

"They knew about Wahlke before he ever got off
that boat," I told him. "You didn't know that? They
watched him get off the boat, been following him ever
since."

"How could they know?" Murray asked. "You don't
have a radio on that boat, and Wahlke would have
blown your head off if you tried to talk to anybody or
became suspicious." He was wiggling around on the
seat, holding his leg. It must have been painful, but he
hadn't yelled since I shot him.

But I had no intention of telling him about the lock
papers, and how I'd put Wahlke and the girl's names on
them and marked them so the tenders would call the

FBI. He was looking worse all the time.

We reached the turnoff Janie indicated, and wound around the farm and residential area near Bothell. Then we turned up a secondary road, and off on to a gravel road, and there was a little private sanitorium. It was all fenced in, with a uniformed private guard at the gate. He looked at something Janie showed him and let us through.

Janie went inside to get an attendant, and I turned back to Murray. "One more thing. How did you know I was an agent? You said Carole didn't think so, but you knew. How?"

In spite of how much it hurt him, he laughed. It wasn't a very pretty laugh because it ended with a groan. "I saw you. At Richmond Landing. Wouldn't have recognized you if I hadn't just been talking about you in Eileen's earlier. What else would you be doing with Ackerman?"

They brought a wheelchair and hustled him into it, and as I watched them take him away I remembered the little man who'd had his throat cut that night Danny was killed.

10

WHEN JANIE CAME out I told her about what he'd said. "This could blow our whole operation up, and your cover too. He's had plenty of time to report that."

She went back inside, and I waited. I found that sitting alone with nothing to do was pretty bad, but I didn't want to talk to Murray anymore. Maybe they wouldn't let me. I hadn't been asked inside. I walked around the grounds inside the wall. Over at one side there was a little creek with a pool in it, and willow trees. I sat and stared at the water and tried to concentrate on watching the little waterfall until Janie came out.

"I think it's okay," she said. "They've put him under to get the bullet out, but before they did he said he hadn't reported you because he wasn't supposed to be near that Richmond Landing operation. He said he got worried about it, and went out to see if the stuff got in all right, but he had orders not to so he never could report seeing you. Then when they got the idea of having you carry the stuff into the country for them, he couldn't tell them why they shouldn't. It was too late, then, to bring out the Richmond Landing business. So he put Wahlke and the girl on your boat to get the heroin off, and sent his man to finish you and Carole. He was going to say he was really after Carole because she fell in love with you and sold out."

"You believe that?" I asked her.

"Yes. It's about the only reasonable explanation of how they got this so fouled up. He's not a real professional agent, Paul. He was agitprop with the Russian group, and when he took China's side they must have promoted him fast. We didn't pull him in because

Shearing thought he wasn't good enough to be much more than agitprop here, but it looks like they used him as a hatchet man. He has the main qualifications for it, anyway. He'll kill. Most of these amateurs they have to work with won't."

I drove us out of the hospital grounds and back toward Seattle. There wasn't any traffic on those back country roads, and I didn't have a wounded man in case I got a ticket, so I really let her out, shifting down to corner and letting the back-end break loose in the gravel. It gave me a few minutes without thinking, and Janie was quiet. I don't think she was worried after the first couple of turns, but maybe she didn't want to distract me. As we pulled onto the highway and I had to go back to normal driving, I said, "Yeah, it's amateur night in the spy business. Murray throws grenades to straighten his mess out with his people, and I shoot them down for you to worry about. Everything's in a mess. I suppose you pros just want to sit back and laugh."

Janie sat up very straight and looked at me while she told me, "I'm not all that much of a professional and you ought to know I don't have ice water for blood. This is my first independent big assignment, and I get just as nervous as you do."

"Sure," I said. "But it's a matter of attitude, isn't it? Like shooting people. I suppose you'd do it if they told you to?"

"I don't know, Paul." She was speaking very softly, saying each word slowly, and she was thinking about it while she talked. "I've never had to. Most of us haven't, you know. You're farther along that way than almost anybody I know, two people in one assignment."

"Yeah. That's my problem, I guess. But both times I was mad at somebody. I didn't have much choice in the matter. But then here's Murray with his professional attitude. Need to get some people out of the way so he sends a guy with a grenade and some hate literature to do it. Carole hadn't done him a damn bit of harm. She wasn't dangerous. But she had to go. That's professional. It scares hell out of me. Do we have professionals like that on our side? I mean, it's one thing to pull the trigger when a man-mountain is bearing down on you, but it's something else to send out a guy with a grenade.''

"What do you suggest we do, Paul? What do you want us to do with John Murray? He'll never be convicted in court. What he told you can't even be mentioned in a courtroom. You don't have one bit of evidence against him, in fact if he gets to the police he could have you charged with kidnapping and assault. Or murder.''

I thought about it as I turned off onto Roosevelt Way. Things had happened so fast I hadn't really considered that in a real sense I was in rebellion against the United States. Oh, sure, I was acting as an agent for one of the departments of government, but the whole government was set up to keep people like us out of it. I could hear King George telling one of his men about how that rabble-rouser Thomas Paine had to be stopped, and there wasn't any law. . . . But Carole was dead. Maybe John Murray hadn't thrown the grenade, but he'd killed her just as sure as if he'd put a rattlesnake in her bed. And there wasn't a way in the world he could be made to pay for it except the way I'd done it.

And there was more to it than that, too. What the hell use were all the laws and rights and the rest of it when, if you tried to cash in on one of them, you were told that the government couldn't help you? Where would any of these fine things be if John Murray and his boys got their way? We could all have fun discussing it wherever they put us before they liquidated us bourgeois degenerates. The hell with it. My job was about over, but I remembered Carole, and the pictures of those kids Harry Shearing had showed me, and I decided I wanted to finish it if I could. They'd let me out now, if I wanted out, but that didn't seem as important as it had. It came to me that somebody had to do this job, and I really wasn't going to be much good for anything until it was done. It was funny, because a couple of days ago I had been ready to take Carole on a long sail down the coast and forget the whole damn thing.

I pulled up in front of a phone booth and told Janie, "Better call the office and see how they're coming on the clean-up job. I'd just as soon not be wanted for murder." She went off to the phone booth, and I slumped back in the seat. It was after two a.m. and I was dead tired. It had been tiring on the boat, and then came all the emotional shocks, action, driving around, and I was beat. Janie was on the phone for a minute or two, then she motioned for me to come take it.

"Larry here," I told it. I didn't recognize the voice on the other end. Why should I, I thought. Shearing, George, and Janie are all I know of this outfit. I filled them in on what had happened and where we took Murray, and I was told that the hospital people took patients and kept their mouths shut, but weren't supposed to know any more than we had to tell them, which was why Janie hadn't invited me in. They didn't need to know who I was.

The guy also let on that Shearing was pretty sure the book George found had the underlings of the dope rackets in it, including some intermediates they wouldn't get in the raid, but probably not the important information on the espionage section. There wasn't any reason why anybody as minor as Roger would have that, although he might have served as liaison with a few. They still hadn't cracked the code in the book, but the experts were hopeful.

"Fine," I told them. "But what interests me is, am I wanted by the homicide squad?"

"No. Nobody called the police, and they won't get it for a while. We've got people going over the place to see if they left anything behind. When they're finished, the Seattle police will be looking for John Murray for the murder of his partner. I doubt that they'll find him. There's no reason for you and your partner to be involved." There was a pause, then the voice said, "Wait one."

It was getting chilly, which isn't surprising for Seattle. A couple of cars drove by the filling station, but nobody paid any attention to a guy and a girl using the telephone. Then Shearing came on the line.

"Larry, it won't be long before Louis and the Treasury boys get their little show on, so we haven't much time before our man hears about it. We may never get him then. You're the only one of my people who knew him. If we do think of something, what part of town is it likely to be in? Out your way?"

"Yeah. He's a District character, so he'd know more places here than anywhere else."

"I thought so," Shearing said. "I'm not doing anything here. Let's have a conference. We might as well make it out there as here, so your place in fifteen minutes. Bring your partner."

I hung up and drove us to my house. What with the grenadier waiting the last time I came home, I was a little worried about going in the place, and left the car a couple of blocks away in a parking lot. We walked around the block, didn't see anything, and got inside fast. Nobody was there, and of course if Murray told it to us straight there wouldn't be, but I made sure the blinds were drawn and the windows locked before I turned on the lights. That would stop a sharpshooter from having a target. There didn't seem to be anything to do about a grenade if the guy didn't mind breaking glass.

Shearing came to the back door a few minutes later. He made some noise opening the porch screen door before he knocked, and I turned out the kitchen lights to see out before I let him in. No question about it, the strain was getting to me. Maybe Janie was feeling something too, because she hadn't said ten words since we got there.

"Still got that Scotch?" he asked. While I was getting it, he said, "Kind of careful coming in, weren't you? Not that I blame you."

"Who's outside?" Janie asked him.

"Doug. I've had him on since before we cleared out last time. That's why I suggested this place to talk; we looked it over before Paul got back and it hasn't been out of sight since. I'm pretty sure it's clean."

"Why watch my house?"

"Somebody else might show up and lead us somewhere. It was as good as having him cruise all over in the hopes he'd see a man he never met, wasn't it? Oh, by the way, here." He handed us each three copies of a photograph of Roger. "Found one in his place and had these made up. Might help. I'll have to turn him in to Louis in the morning anyway, I guess. Can't take a chance on him blowing out and nobody getting him. Wish we could, though."

We sat around my dining room table. Janie had discovered my beer cooler, and Shearing and I started on a second Scotch. He took out a little notebook and began ticking off points as he talked.

"Let's see what we've got. Paul tells us he's an egotistical incompetent, no friends, bores people stiff. He shows up to inspect Paul after John Murray got the idea of using him, and ends up suggesting that the girl go on the trip. No evidence that the girl knew he was one of theirs, but none that she didn't either. He didn't let her see him in Victoria, but he did stay in the terminal while she made the pickup. From where he was, he could watch her go back to your boat, right? You can see the visitors' dock from the observation deck of the terminal?" I nodded, and he went on. "That's the last we know of him. The records show he didn't take a car into Canada, so he went on the ferry. He may not have stayed at all, just come right back after the pickup. He won't leave Vancouver Island by any normal means now; they kept copies of those pictures and they're looking for him now that he's identified. The point is, is there any reason he would know we're looking for him?"

"Not if Murray was telling the truth," Janie told him. "But would he have known what Murray was planning with the grenade? Would hearing about an explosion this close to Paul's house have scared him into hiding?"

"We'll keep that as a suggestion to come back to."

Shearing made a note in his book and started a doodle. This one resembled a map of an island with fortifications that kept becoming more and more elaborate. He drew in a gun emplacement and said, "According to Murray, everybody else in the organization who knew about it approved the idea of Paul's bringing the stuff in for them. You can figure why it would be perfect material for blackmail after it was safe. Murray knew Paul was something more than he seemed to be, so he had to arrange a stunt. He sends a man who just came up from L.A. a week before Murray got here which indicates that he was one of Murray's people rather than part of the local organization. Do both of you buy that story?"

I thought about it for a minute. "Yeah, I think I do. John's tough and when I knew him he was reasonably sharp, but he never thought about lock papers. He hadn't been here for so long he forgot about them, if he ever knew. So he figures Wahlke can keep watch on me and scrub me if he thinks I'm wise to anything. After I drop them off the grenade gets me, and nobody ever finds anything that indicates heroin was involved. Yeah, it's just the kind of damn fool desperate stunt he might try if he got rattled. But that means Roger thinks he's safe. Unless he's just playing it smart and keeping out of sight until he gets word the stunt came off. Maybe he's watching to see that the distribution gang gets the stuff before he goes home. I think I would."

"Sure," Janie said. "Lots of pushers are on the junk themselves. They don't know anything about China and wouldn't care anyway, but if they ran short they'd start looking for their supplier. But they wouldn't know Balsinger, so why should he hide from them?"

"Maybe that's it, and maybe it's the explosion," Shearing said. "The pushers wouldn't know him, but this thing's not that deep and Balsinger's not that big. One or two of them might know somebody who does know Balsinger, and if he's running scared he might keep out of the way for a day or so until he knows it worked. So it may not be us he's hiding from, and then he might not be hiding at all. He may just be out of town. But I don't think so, not with this operation going on. He'd want to be somewhere he could keep an eye on things, get messages from maybe one man, things like that. Now where would that be?''

"His office?" I suggested. Shearing shook his head. "I've had that gone over already," he told us. We thought about it some more, and I got myself a glass of beer. Three Scotches in my condition would finish me off. I tried to think where Roger would go. Someplace he'd be safe, and where he could come back from if everything was all right. It had to be someplace he'd go normally.

"Did anybody check out Balsinger's folks?" I asked.

"Not directly. We can't go bothering people like that on Sunday night. Louis could, but he'd want to know why. We called their house and asked for Roger, but whoever answered the phone said he hadn't been there for a month. I thought you said his parents had disowned him."

"Just with money," I told them. "Roger's still their only kid, and they keep hoping he'll grow up. He goes out to be nice to them five or six times a year."

"How do we know," Janie asked, "that he isn't spending the night with some girl?"

"If you knew Roger you wouldn't ask. The only way he ever gets a girl to go out with him is to impress her with his car and his beach house." I broke it off as I thought about it. "The damn beach house! He's got the use of a place his folks own out on the Sound. It's not too far, either. Maybe that's it."

Shearing stood up. "It's worth a try. I'll stay here, and you take Doug and Janie out to check it over. Remember, we want him alive." He looked straight at me. "If possible, we would also like him without bullet holes in his leg too."

I grinned. I felt good. I had a job to do, and somebody seemed to think I could do it. Just what every kid wants to be.

Janie made the same arm signal Shearing had given back at Roger's apartment, and a little guy with horn-rimmed glasses and buckteeth showed up just as we got to my car. He wasn't as ugly as you thought at first glance, but he sure wasn't any Cary Grant. He looked like a skinny little accountant who didn't get enough exercise.

As we got in, Janie said, "Paul, meet Doug. Quiet night, wasn't it?"

His voice surprised me. With the rest of him so funny-looking, I expected something unusual about that too, but it was just a voice. "Yeah, quiet. Sorry about the girl, Paul. I saw the guy run to the car, but he was on the wrong side for a shot. Nothing I could do. I would have collared him, but Alessandro come busting out, and it figured I could let him handle it. Alessandro don't know me. What now?"

As I eased the car out of the lot, Janie told him. "Paul thinks he may know where Balsinger is, and we're going to look."

"Sure beats hell out of watching your house all night. Figure it's safe to leave the chief alone in there?"

"Oh, you don't know about that, do you? Paul caught the man who ordered the grenade, and we think he was the only one on to us." Janie laughed. "And I feel sorry for anybody who wants Mr. Shearing."

We drove out 45th through Ballard. The beach house wasn't far from where the canal opened into the Sound. Like a lot of places along there, the house itself wasn't much, but the land underneath was worth more than I'd ever make in my life. We crossed over the Ballard Bridge and went on westward toward Fort Lawton. I remembered Carole used to go demonstrate in front of Fort Lawton, until the peace crowd found out the only thing there was an air defense computer. They were fooled because the Army called it a "Missile Master."

The house is on a bluff looking down at the canal. It has a view of the locks and Shilshole Marina, and you can sit on the sundeck and watch the ships come in and out. Roger used to have little parties there, and the place is so nice it was worth going to even though you had to listen to Roger. Well, worth it once in a while. Roger's friends had run to the drippy set, undergraduates and people he could impress, but he'd invite anybody he thought was respectable.

You can't drive right up to the house. There's a dirt driveway you can use when it's dry, but in Seattle that almost never happens, so you have to park at the bottom of the hill and walk up. There's a carport down there, and I took a look inside, then waved to the others.

"That's his car," I told them.

"Pretty snazzy," Janie said. "A silver TR4. I wouldn't mind having that."

"Neither would I. But maybe he got a lemon, the thing's in the shop half the time," I told her. I gave them my best sour grapes look.

"I guess you're supposed to be in charge," Janie told me, "but maybe Doug ought to organize this."

"All right by me," I said. "The house has two entrances. One is at ground level just at the end of this path. Well, almost ground level, there's a couple of steps. That leads to a living room. The other entrance is up some stairs over to the left as we face the house, and it lets you in the kitchen. There are two bedrooms on the back side with a little central hall that connects with all four rooms, and there's a daylight basement fixed up as a game room under the kitchen. Roger usually uses the right-hand bedroom. Oh, and you see the deck there. It runs right around the house on three sides."

"We'll do this simple," Doug said. "Paul, you know him, so you knock on the front door. Be ready to hit him with something hard. I'll get behind the house and go in a bedroom window while he's answering the door. Janie can cover the door on the other side. Okay?" We nodded. "Give me a few minutes to get in back."

We struggled through the mud and up the hill, and I waited for the others to reach position. Janie took her gun out, and I noted that I'd been right. She kept it in a little holster strapped low on the inside of her left thigh. You had quite a view when she drew it.

When they were all set, I rang the doorbell. Nothing happened. I rang it again, then pounded on the door.

There might have been a noise inside, and there might not. I pounded some more then I heard something around the corner to my left. I jumped down two steps and ran around the corner just in time to see Roger taking off down the hill. He'd gone out on the deck and jumped the eight feet or so to the ground. He had shoes and trousers on, and a coat, but his pajama tops were sticking out under the coat. He was carrying what looked like a briefcase.

I cocked the pistol and aimed at his legs. The gun made enough noise to wake everybody in town, but he didn't stop. Then I ran after him, hit the mud in the driveway, and went on my face. As I got up, I heard his car start.

It was fifty or sixty feet to the carport from where I was, and he was pulling out when I reached there. I had to jump to keep from being run down, and he was off.

A Barracuda doesn't have the turning radius of a true sports car, but she'll do a U-turn on most streets. I got her started and around, and couldn't see Janie and Doug, so I wound her up. Roger's little Triumph would do tricks my buggy couldn't dream of, but on the other hand the acceleration of my big 4 bbl. Detroit gas eater isn't anything to sneeze at. I was doing sixty in fifteen seconds, then braking for the sharp turn onto the asphalt.

Roger didn't have any choice as to where to go. There is only one through-street from where he was to the rest of the city, and it doesn't wind much. My car isn't as good as his, but I knew I was a better driver than Roger. He'd once tried to take his then-current Singer around the track at Shelton after a race, and spun out twice. He'd be more careful than me. I was pushing a hundred in half a minute, and damn glad for the Formula S package. Those Blue Streak tires are advertised as the best road holding jobs made for a production car, and I'll give the Goodyear people a testimonial any day they ask for it.

By the time I reached any turnoffs, I could see him ahead of me. He had distinctive taillights, and it was a relief to see I hadn't lost him. Then I poured it on, and began catching up.

The road twists down the side of Magnolia Bluff after you get away from the fort, and his car had all the advantages there, with its low center of gravity and quick steering, but he was cornering sloppily. When he missed a shift, I thought I had him, but that beautiful piece of mechanism saved it for him. We shot across the valley and down the causeway, and there we were, on a freeway stretch that runs to the Ballard Bridge. Just short of the bridge, he cut off to the right and headed along the base of Queen Anne Hill, and I closed up to forty feet or so of him. The problem was, what to do now. I didn't trust my shooting, and at that speed if I hit him anywhere he'd be dead anyway. In a few minutes, the police were going to get into the act, and since I was in the tail car, they might stop me and not him. I figured to try a stunt you see in movies, but nobody in his right mind would do, namely cut him off and force him over. Roger always was chicken, and maybe he hadn't been putting on such an act. I hoped not, anyway, because if he just held straight we'd both be meat.

We tore down the hill past Seattle Pacific College, and I kept edging up to try it. Whenever I'd get close, he'd get enough guts to floor it and swing across the road, forcing me back and about then my nerve would give just enough, and he'd be off again. We played tag all down that hill, then around a wide sweeping curve and up to the approach to the Fremont Bridge. I thought he was going past it and up Queen Anne Hill, but when he'd almost passed the bridge he threw that little bug sharp left and drifted a nice turn.

There wasn't any time for calculation. He'd be away from me if he got across while I had to turn around. I didn't give it any thought, I just twisted the wheel, slammed the brake enough to break loose, and brought that beautiful transmission into second. Then it was a question of which would happen first, the wheels having traction or the car going sideways through the bridge railing. When I gained control again I had some more reasons to be thankful for the tires, not to mention the posi-traction rear end. Detroit does make some good machinery, even if the stylists get in the way of the engineers once in a while.

Roger blew it when he was across. He turned up a dead end. I didn't figure he knew that's what it was, but the street leads to some dirt under the Aurora high bridge, and nothing else. The Barracuda had lost some ground in that turning duel, putting me forty or fifty yards behind Roger when I lost sight of him, but at the speed we were making that wouldn't be much time. He was out of sight for maybe twenty seconds. Then I saw the TR coming to a stop under the bridge.

His car looked empty. There wasn't any place he could have gone to, but I didn't see him. I got out and ran over to the Triumph, and when I looked around it for him, I heard him behind me.

"Drop it, and stand still, Paul," he said. I turned to face where I heard him, but I couldn't see a thing. He was outside the pool of light coming down from the street lamps on the bridge sixty feet above us, while I was right in it.

"Drop it, Paul. I won't tell you again."

There wasn't much to get behind. It seemed like a hell of a thing to do after chasing him that far, but what else was there? I let the hammer down on the pistol and tossed it out in front of me.

He was lying in the dirt just outside the light. I didn't see him until he got up, and from where he was he could have hit me six times before I had a chance. He must have dived out over the top of his little bug and let it roll on, counting on the slight incline to stop it. That way he ended up behind where I thought he'd be. Well, short of letting him get away, I didn't see what else I could have done.

"Okay, what now?" I asked him. I could figure he didn't want any noise if he could help it, and if he got close enough I might have a chance.

"Now we take a walk. In case you're trying to make plans, I'd better tell you something. I don't think I can get out of this, but you're all I have right now. Before they kill me, I'll make sure you're dead. If they don't get me, you might get out of this alive. It's a slim hope, but it's all you have."

"Yeah, Roger. Come down to it, neither one of us has a chance. They'll turn the city over looking for you."

"Enough talking. Stand right over there while I get something. If you look this way I'll shoot you. I'm afraid of you, Paul, and I don't intend to let you get me." He went over toward his car. There was enough of an edge to his voice that I didn't want to test him. The little bastard was cornered, and I didn't know what he'd do. I was more worried about him getting away than what he'd do to me. That wasn't courage, it was just that I couldn't get used to thinking of Roger as anything more than a boob.

He got his briefcase or whatever it was out of the car, and switched off the lights of both vehicles. "Now walk. That way." He motioned me off to the right, toward the University District. "Just walk," he told me. "I'll tell you where to turn. Keep your hands where I can see them, and remember, if you give somebody a signal I'll shoot you first and worry about them later."

We headed east and south toward the old gasworks. He could shoot off a cannon there and nobody would pay any attention. I tried to get him talking on the way, but he growled at me to shut up or he'd crack me across the head, and it seemed he might mean it. We walked about a mile, and the sky was starting to get gray when we reached the little cove next to the gasworks. There are houseboats there. It was also where I kept *Witch of Endor*.

"You see, Paul, you are going to help me. You're going to take me up the Sound and out toward the ocean. They may be watching my boat, but I'll bet they won't be looking for yours. Now get aboard."

Once on *Witch*, he made me strip to the skin. While I spreadeagled myself on the double berth, he went through my clothes and took everything out of my pockets. Then he let me dress again. It was getting light fast by the time all this was over.

"Get moving. Come on, get this damn boat headed out," he said. There was that same desperate quality in his voice. The guy was about to give up and before he did he'd shoot.

Once I got the boat moving he went below. "Sit where I can see you. When we get to the locks, you say one word and both you and the tender are finished. The only way you can help them get me is to kill yourself. It's all up to you."

He put the gun down and started messing with the stove to make coffee. By the time I could get close to him, he could have picked the thing up and shot off the full string so there wasn't any point in trying. I had another plan in mind anyway, so I acted cooperative. We motored down the lake.

The Fremont Bridge opened at my signal, and I looked up at where we'd been not long before. The canal was too deep to see our cars. By the time we got through the bridge, the coffee was ready. Roger poured me a cup, but he kept it until it got lukewarm before he'd give it to me. Hell, I wouldn't have thrown it at him. I needed the coffee just to stay awake.

As we came into the locks he gave his spiel again. "Remember, one word to the tender and you both get it. Maybe you don't care about you, but think of his wife and kids. And here—leave this where I can see it until you give it to him." He handed me a lock paper. He must have found mine in the cabin and filled one out while I was drinking the coffee. There went the plan I'd had.

It took forever to get through that damn lock. The tender was friendly and cheerful, chatted about the weather, which was going to be good for sailing up the Sound, and with Roger sitting down there, nervous as hell, that was the last thing I needed. When I went forward to fix up the bow line, Roger came out into the cockpit and handed the tender the lock paper. I hadn't had a chance to mark it.

"Sure going to be a beautiful day for a cruise," the tender told us. "You boys are headed for Victoria, eh? That's a nice trip. Wish I could head out on a Monday morning. Mind the weather tonight, hear there's going to be a blow." He cast the line off. "Good luck," he shouted after us. Roger got back in the cabin when I took the tiller, and we headed off into the Sound.

We motored on out and headed north. I was about to pass out at the tiller, and told Roger that he might as well get it done with, because I wasn't going to steer any more.

"Oh, that's all right, Paul. I could use some company. You just sit up against the cabin there and I'll take it. I don't know much about sailing, but with a motor anybody can hold a tiller. I'll wake you up when the wind comes up."

"How in hell did you get in this racket?" I asked him. "I thought you were too smart for this crap. You can't possibly believe in it as some kind of cause, you never believed in a cause in your life." I settled myself against the aft side of the cabin and tried to get comfortable, while he took the tiller. He put his gun in his belt after I was well sprawled out. The cockpit is better than six feet long, which was a long way to jump from a prone position.

"You ought to have joined yourself, Paul. You could be a big man. When they told me they might be able to recruit you, I knew better than to swallow that line about how you were beginning to believe, but I thought you'd be smart enough to see the advantages. I even had it in mind to make you my second in command. I liked you, Paul. You didn't slap me around, and you even stood up for me when somebody else did. Why'd you have to go and ruin everything?"

I gave him a sick grin. "I didn't know it was you, you know. Maybe I'd have been more interested if I had. I thought those losers were running the show. No point in getting in on an operation where you have to be a true believer to get ahead. How'd you manage that?"

"It's easy to make those guys believe anything. You'd be surprised how many there are like me in the movement. But I was different. Most of them were scared of what they were doing. I'm a realist. If something had to be done, I did it. It didn't take long for them to realize how valuable I could be. There aren't many in the state more important to them than I am.''

"Yeah, I found that out," I told him. "You can still be a big man, you know. Think about it. If you join up with us, you can show how to catch everybody in the state. After that's done, maybe they'll send you overseas. The only thing against you that would stand up in court would be holding a gun on me right now, and that's easy to take care of. What could they convict you of?"

"Come off it, Paul. You think I don't know what happens to people like me? Courts, huh. You know damn well I'd be more likely to end up in the Sound with an anchor around my feet and my belly slit open so I wouldn't float. Maybe there would have been a chance, but not now. You'd kill me yourself to get even for Carole if you could."

He startled me. "Carole? John Murray had Carole killed. He did it on his own. What did you have to do with that?"

"You didn't know? John ordered it done, but he couldn't give an order like that without my permission. He told me all about how she was in love with you, and how you felt about the dope racket, and how she was beginning to think there was something besides film in those cans. So I let him go ahead with it. When I looked out the window and saw it was you knocking on the door, I thought you knew and were there to kill me. Weren't you? What were you doing there, anyway? Didn't Murray talk?"

I didn't say anything. It was coming to me that Roger might not know anybody was after him except me, in which case he was just taking me for a ride out in the Sound. His description of what Shearing's boys would do to him would fit me just as well.

"Didn't Murray talk?" Roger shouted. "Damn it, you went in his house and came out with him limping. You shot him and killed his buddy. Didn't he tell you about me?"

"He told me you were the one who had the bright idea about getting me to smuggle narcotics into the country, Roger. That's all he told me. I resent hell out of being used that way and I went to see you, that's all."

"Doesn't matter. I guess it's all over now. That blonde girl you run around with knows. I thought you liked Carole, you know that? I thought you and Carole were real thick. She thought so, that's why I let Murray go ahead. And here you show up with that blonde before they finish cleaning Carole up off the sidewalk. I got to hand it to you, you sure can collect them. You had Carole all sewed up too. I went to see her just before you left on that trip and she wouldn't even talk to me. If she only knew who sent her to you in the first place, she'd have known how important I was. She'd have talked to me then."

We were a good way out in the Sound by then, heading north-northwest in the general direction of Admiralty Inlet. He made me get his little briefcase affair out for him, watching me so closely I didn't have a chance to do anything else. He took a reel of wire out of it, and after he told me what he wanted I got it attached to a halyard and pulled an end up the mast. There was a microphone and headset in the little leather case.

"Laurie J, this is Alfred. Laurie J, this is Alfred," he told it. He kept that up for a couple of minutes, then said, "I have transportation. I have excess baggage. Where can you meet me for some real fishing? I have a bait with extra secret ingredients. Over." He listened some more, then put all the gear back in the briefcase. "You be good, Paul, and you can live the rest of the day anyway. They'll meet us before dark off Dungeness, and then I suppose we'll have to sink your boat with you in it."

"Yeah. Well, if it's all the same to you, Roger, I didn't get to bed last night. I think I'll go to sleep." He didn't say anything, mostly because he didn't believe me. But the one thing I learned in the army was to sleep anywhere, anytime, in any position. I won't say I actually slept soundly, but I managed to get some rest. I figured he'd be waking me up in about three hours, and it was a long way to Dungeness Spit.

11

IT DIDN'T TAKE three hours. Roger was running the motor full throttle, and that eats gas. The engine in *Witch* is like a lot of sailboat engines, there's too much horsepower for the boat. A sailboat has a hull speed, and no matter how fast you run the motor, after it reaches that speed it won't go faster. You just use the extra power making big waves. I had been running low on fuel after the trip, but hadn't bothered to get more because we hadn't needed it. Running at max engine revs, it lasted no more than a couple of hours. I woke up when the engine missed, caught, missed again, sputtered, and died out.

Roger had a helpless look on his face. I actually felt sorry for him, but not much. "What's the matter with this thing?" he yelled.

"Out of fuel, I suppose. Ran her pretty low on the trip."

He looked desperate. When he looked around, then pointed the gun at me, I thought I had better do something.

"This is a sailboat, and there's a wind. If you'll let me get the blasted sails up, you can still make your appointment. There's a good southeast wind, right off our quarter, and she'll go like a bat. Faster than with the engine." ●

He lowered the gun. "Get them up. You try anything and I'll kill you. I need you to get this thing going, but I guess I could figure out how to sail it if I had to."

I doubted that, but didn't see any point in telling him. He'd find out soon enough. Getting a sailboat under way in a brisk wind, without power to hold steerage way until the main is up, is not so easy. With a complete lubber for a helmsman, it's damn near impossible. The main kept getting fouled on the spreaders, and Roger didn't know how to let her fall off, gather way, and point back up into the wind again. I had to keep shouting at him what to do, and pull the halyard by myself since he wasn't about to put his gun down. I wasn't in too much of a hurry anyway, so it took over fifteen minutes. Once the main was up, we got the staysail and jib set without too much trouble.

The wind was off our starboard quarter, and it had blown up to twenty knots while we were motoring. There was a good sea running along with us, and Roger found that he simply couldn't steer. The boat kept wallowing from side to side, almost dipping the boom in the water as it rolled, and threatened to broach. After a couple of minutes of this he told me to take the helm.

Then there was nothing to do but sail. We were making good speed, at least six knots and probably more with surfing down the whitecaps, and it was a lot of fun. Or it would have been a lot of fun if it hadn't been for Roger and his gun. I wasn't all that worried about him now. He needed me to get to his friends, while I could always manage to stop him from getting there. For that matter, once we were in Admiralty I could dive overboard. The boat would roll, Roger couldn't chase me because he couldn't handle her, and it wouldn't be too far to shore. Cold, yes, but I should be able to handle that.

There was only one trouble. By the time we reached Admiralty Inlet, off Point No Point, my arms were so tired I didn't think I could stay afloat long enough to make shore. Hanging onto the tiller of a sailboat in a following sea is work. I was beginning to believe in wheel steering, although most sailboat men would rather not have them because they aren't sensitive enough or quick enough in emergencies.

I had another thing to think about too. Roger didn't know that my boat was paid for by Shearing and Company, so he hadn't thought about the fact that they ought to be looking for me pretty quick, and know just where to look. He evidently thought I was just what I seemed to be, a guy who didn't like dope smuggling and got mad. He was running out because I got to Murray. I made sure by getting him to talk some more.

"Yeah, Paul, I guess it's all over. After your girl friend gets through talking they'll be looking for me for smuggling narcotics, and it won't take the counterspies long to connect dope and Murray's politics. So even if I can't be convicted in court, they'll get me. One way or another, they take care of people like me. You didn't know that, did you? That there are government people who make people disappear? Well, there are."

"Where are you going, Roger?" I asked him.

"Oh, they'll have a use for me somewhere. There aren't many people who can get them to help when real trouble starts. A fishing boat will get me and take me to another boat, and I'll end up somewhere in Canada. Different name, new passport, it won't be hard to go somewhere."

"You must be important to be worth all that trouble. If it was me in your fix, I'd worry about my friends drowning me to shut me up. You sure they won't?"

"Now why would they do that?" There was a trace of fear in his voice, and he started talking to make himself feel better. "I've done a lot for them. I got narcotics into the country, I recruited pushers, I even helped them get rid of some gangsters who didn't want competition. I've done a lot for them. They won't let me down."

"So had Leon Trotsky," I said. "Oh, excuse me, wrong outfit. Let's see, I'm not up on my Chinese Communism. Who's been purged lately?"

I didn't hear what he said next, because we were almost swamped by a wake from a big power cruiser that had pulled up behind us. It roared by and the helmsman waved at us in a peculiar way. I didn't get it at first, but then it came to me. He had waved the same way that Shearing had when he signaled Janie, and the same way Janie had summoned Doug. I couldn't make out the features of the three men and a girl in the boat because they were bundled up, a little too bundled up for summer even in Seattle. The only face I had seen at all, now that I thought of it, was the helmsman, and that might or might not have been George, but I would have bet that girl had blonde curly hair under the hood of her parka. So now I had reinforcements. I couldn't see how they'd do me a lot of good. Accurate shooting at any range at all would be nearly impossible the way the boats were pitching around in the riptides. Admiralty is famous for the things. They also made it impossible for me to jump overboard until slack water, which wouldn't be for a couple of hours. When I was thinking about jumping before, I hadn't known what the tides would be. So they couldn't shoot Roger from their boat, and I couldn't jump. Come right down to it, they wouldn't shoot him anyway. They'd want him alive.

Their boat was one of those chrome and mahogany twin-screw power jobs that can make over twenty knots, if you don't mind wasting fuel. They were doing twelve or so now, so it didn't take long for them to get past. We were coming off Bush Point, and it figured that they would go on up into Admiralty Bay and wait to see what we were doing.

Roger didn't look too good. He couldn't have had a lot of sleep the night before either, since he knew I'd been to Murray's place. I wondered how he knew that. Ron maybe. Didn't think Ron had it in him to put down his bottle after what had happened.

I could see how I might manage to get Roger's gun out of the way, and with the crew nearby I wasn't too worried about whatever would meet him. The problem now was to hang on long enough to get there. It was a little easier in the Inlet, the wind had shifted more easterly and was now off the beam rather than behind us, but it was still a strain to hold on. I balanced her off a bit with the foresails so I could let go of the blasted tiller once in a while, and talked Roger out of a shot of rum. He had one too, and I thought for a minute that might be the easy way to do it, but of course he wasn't that dumb.

I got him to fill up a big glass with rum and pineapple juice, and settled down for the long haul. We rounded Point Wilson about four in the afternoon, and headed west toward Dungeness. The wind was dead aft now, and *Witch* rolled her guts out. Everything in the cabin came loose and flew in the bilges, and the wind kept getting stronger and stronger. We had a foul tide as well, so that the seas built up, and the little tide rips in the banks off Protection Island were crossways to the seas, so that it got hairy. I should have reduced sail, but in the first place it would have been pretty good reason for wanting the boat as hard to handle as possible.

"Better break out the life jackets, Roger," I told him. He didn't think much of the idea. "Look, man," I said, "in this weather anything could happen. Ah, forget it." He didn't forget it, though. He put one of the orange horsecollars on. I didn't get one, but then from his point of view it didn't matter anyway. I wanted him to be wearing one for reasons of my own.

Well up ahead of us, the big powerboat put into the little bay behind Dungeness Light. That got them out of the wind, but it also got them a long way from the action. Of course they didn't know we were getting close to the rendezvous point, and they'd be worried about Roger seeing them. This way we would be past them and they could follow us again.

I looked to see if Roger had spotted the cruiser, but he was getting seasick. It didn't figure that he would notice anything going on around him. He turned a deathly green, and from the time it happened to me I knew how he felt. I thought I might be able to get the gun once he really got sick, but he kept pulling himself together so I couldn't make a try. An hour and a half of fighting nausea took all the alertness out of him, but it also made him more edgy and desperate than ever.

We passed Dungeness Light a little before six, and Roger told me to follow the spit. Dungeness Spit is a five mile sandbar sticking northeastwards from the Olympic Peninsula. It's about twenty miles east of Port Angeles, and there's absolutely nothing on it but sand. In fact, there's nothing around there at all. Old Dungeness and the Indian village of Jamestown are on the east side of the base of the hook, and you can't see over the spit from ground level, even though the thing's only about thirty feet out of the water. The light is at the end of the spit and there may be a light tender to take care of the radio beacon, but I don't know. It's certainly not an observation post. I think they take care of it by boat from Point Wilson twenty miles to the east. The area west of Dungeness, where we were headed, is absolutely wild. At the base of the spit the land rises fast so that there's a bluff at the edge of the water. All you can see at the top of the bluff is trees. In the right season, you can cruise around in this area and not see a living soul for weeks. It's never got too many boats near the land anyway, because the big ships coming to Seattle stay to the middle of the channel. If you want to commit a murder, Dungeness Spit is as good a place for it as any.

It happened that I had been out there not too long before which was why I knew so much about it. The fact that I had sailed a lot in these regions was probably the deciding factor in my client getting me, but at any rate he was putting in a summer house and wanted me to design him a pier that could take the pounding weather. I did, but it cost him a lot of money. His place was up on the cliff above the water, a summer house, and while I was out inspecting the pier he was trying to clear out some of the trees. They were huge things, with stumps rooted deep in the ground, and I showed him how to dynamite them once the trees were cut. Bulldozers are wonderful, but you couldn't get one to his place. There was no road whatever, and he didn't want one. You reached his place by water, putting in at the pier I designed, and went up a steep stairway to the top of the forty-foot cliff. In addition to dynamiting his stumps, I'd rigged a hoist for him so he could get his building materials up to the level of his house. He'd always wanted to build his own house, and this was going to be it.

It was a long way from blasting stumps to fighting the tiller with a gun pointed at me. Roger was beginning to feel better now that we were taking the seas off the quarter, and I was getting nervous. This was where his friends would be; now where were mine? I didn't want to look behind me much, but I mumbled something about what kind of seas were building up back there, and turned around. There was no sign of the power-boat, but off the starboard quarter a fishing boat was coming up on us. It was a standard Seattle fish boat, big tubby thing made out of two layers of three-inch plank-ing, huge Diesel engine, and two big fishing poles with hydraulic gurdies. They have aft cockpits where you can control the boat as well as from the wheelhouse, because the same man handles the fish as well as steers. One or two men go out on these things and stay all season, going to port only long enough to unload the fish and get more ice and fuel. If they don't make a good catch, they don't go in.

It isn't that unusual to see one in the Straits in sum-mer, but they aren't common either. The owner-cap-tains like to be out where the fishing is, and they won't come in farther than Neah Bay unless there's repairs to make that can't be done on the coast. This one being here at the time Roger was expecting somebody was a little too convenient.

Those fishing boats don't do much more than eight or ten knots, and we were making better than six, so it would take him at least half an hour to close the two miles between us. That was all right with me, it gave Janie and her friends time to be on the scene. Not seeing them, though, I was beginning to have some doubts about whether or not it was really them. It should have been them. It would take some time to find my car where I left it, but even if Shearing didn't want to broadcast an alarm for Roger he could give the police my car's description. Once they knew we weren't in the automobiles, it shouldn't have taken him long to check the fact that the boat was gone and send somebody out. He might even have come himself. That all sounded great, and there had been that arm signal, but it looked awful lonesome out on the Straits.

Roger finally saw the fishing boat. It took him long enough, but I put that down to the green in his complex-ion. When he saw it, he asked me, "How do you turn on the lights in this thing?"

I tried to stall, but he got that desperate look and demanded again.

"Right down there below where you're sitting, on the side of the bridge deck," I told him. "Yeah, that's the switch."

He turned the lights on, checked to see they were lit, and blinked them three times. The red port bow light of the fish boat flashed, and Roger said, "Slow this thing down. Here, get the sails down."

This was it, I figured. "Hang on a second, I have to turn in front of the wind. You want to take the tiller while I get the sails off? Sailboats don't stop in a high wind, you know—if you just let go of the tiller she'll roll over and dismast herself."

He didn't know what to do. He believed me, because it had scared him when the boat rolled and put the boom nearly in the water back in the Inlet, so he knew if he shot me before the sails were off there was a chance bad things would happen to him. While he was making up his mind I got the wind right aft, and let her roll a bit. "If I let go of this thing now you'll sink before your buddies ever get close," I shouted. "Get back here and take this if you want us to go slower. I can't slow down with all this sail up."

It was blowing hard, and the seas were building up behind *Witch*. She'd surf down one, shooting ahead, and climb up the next. Each time she'd surf she'd go as fast as the water, and the rudder wouldn't bite, so I'd lose control for a second. The sails would drive her toward the wind, and I'd have to strain to bring her back on course. It was exciting, and it was also a bit dangerous. I'd have reefed the main and brought in the jib if I'd been alone, but I wanted things as hairy as possible when the moment came.

Roger made up his mind, and stood to come aft. He was concentrating on me, and while he was watching I put the tiller over to weather. *Witch* came right around, her stern went through the wind, and just as Roger took a step toward me the wind caught the main and swept the boom across the deck. It caught Roger on the shoulder, knocking him over to the rail, and the boat, caught broadside to the wind, heeled just as he came up against the lifelines.

He might have made it if he'd let go the gun. The stupid fool tried to keep it instead of grabbing with both hands, and the boom swept him right into the water.

I noted that the boat still had a mast. Hitting Roger must have slowed the boom enough to keep it from slamming to a stop with enough force to pull the stick out of her. I still wasn't out of trouble, though. The end of the boom dug into the water, and the rudder couldn't hold her. I frantically pulled in on the mainsheet, thankful for the two double blocks in the system. As we went through another jibe, I got some line in so that it wasn't so bad. I still had that sailboat all over the Straits, and the two foresails up didn't help a bit either, but things were a little more under control. After the second jibe, I let her come on up into the wind, hauling the boom in as fast as I could, and got her onto a beat. Then I adjusted the foresails, put the helm down, and tacked, leaving the staysail cleated to windward. I'd lied to Roger about not being able to stop a sailboat in the wind, of course. Sailboats have been heaving to for centuries, and while some modern yachts won't do it, a cutter almost always will. The theory is that the sails cancel each other out. Hove to, the tiller could be lashed down to leeward and she'd handle herself long enough for me to do something about all that sail area.

I ran forward and got the jib set to windward, cleated it, and took the staysail down. I didn't do anything fancy, just lashed it with the bow mooring line I'd left coiled around the cleat. I'd rather have had a good stormsail set where the staysail was, and get the jib off entirely, but I didn't have much choice. Once the staysail was down, though, *Witch* heeled a lot less hove to, and I could sail her.

I put her into the wind, looking for Roger. With his life jacket on he had a chance, and when he went over I'd thrown him a seat cushion, one of those floating things the Coast Guard grudgingly approves in lieu of real life preservers. There was a slim chance I'd find him.

The fishing boat was closing fast, and I wasn't about to let those guys catch me if I could help it. *Witch* couldn't outrun them, but she could sure get to shore before they caught me. It was less than a mile to the end of the spit, and the shore wasn't very inviting, but it was the only thing I could think of to do.

I still wanted to find Roger, though. Shearing wanted to talk to him, and I owed him something too. We were out of the tide rips, so he had a chance, even if it wasn't a very good one. I tacked upwind, trying to follow the reverse of the course I had been steering when he went over. The trouble was that I wasn't too sure what course that was. The pair of uncontrolled jibes, plus the time I had spent hove to so I could get the boat in a condition I could handle, had made it hopeless to simply sail back up my own wake, even if that had been possible. With all the wind and that much sail up, *Witch* was heeled over with her lee rail almost under. I would have liked to have a reef in the main, but that would have taken fifteen minutes or so, and he would have been long gone by then, even if his friends hadn't caught me.

I saw the cushion. There wasn't a sign of anybody near it. Thinking it might have drifted faster than he did, I went upwind of it as best I could. The fishing boat was less than half a mile away, and closing fast now that I wasn't moving away from it. I could make out a shape a mile or so behind that, and the red-green lights told me it was headed straight for me. I decided to take a chance on it being some of Shearing's gang, so I made another quick search, shouting for Roger.

I thought I heard something. I thought I might just have heard somebody call my name. It was hard to tell. With the boat close-hauled the wind screamed in the rigging and was trying to tear my head off. It must have been hitting thirty to thirty-five knots in the gusts, and *Witch* was heeling over so far water came over the coaming into the cockpit until I'd luff her up and spill the wind out of the sails. Each time I'd do that in those seas, I'd nearly lose control because she lost speed fast. There was just too much sail up for windward work, and if anything the wind was becoming stronger. Whitecaps were everywhere, and every third or fourth wave was a real breaker. Salt spray blew in my eyes, making it even harder to see, and it was getting dark faster and faster now. I could be in real trouble whether the fishing boat caught me or not. Without lights it might not be able to see me, but I couldn't count on it. Some of those things have surplus radar sets the fishermen rebuild and install, and if this one did they could follow me almost to shore.

Green water broke over the bow, half tearing the lashed-down staysail loose, and washing a hundred pounds of water across the top of the cabin. Most of it poured in through the open companionway slide, but several gallons got me as well. That did it. If I waited any longer I'd have to heave to and reef, and they'd be on me in minutes. That might or might not be Shearing's people in the cruiser, but it wouldn't matter to me. Roger's friends would remember his remarks about excess baggage, and they might do something about it. They'd have no reason to believe the power cruiser was anything other than a pleasure yacht out to make Port Angeles in time for a late dinner.

It was tricky enough bringing *Witch* around before the wind again. I didn't particularly want to be broadside to a breaking sea like the one that wet me down. If it hit just right there was a chance it could tear something loose, like the cabin sides for example. It probably wouldn't, certainly no sea built up by that kind of wind could, but in the Straits the seas aren't just built up by the winds. The tides have a lot to do with it, and I've seen real breakers in twenty knots of wind out there. I brought her around between breaking waves, getting a little more water over the coamings in the process. The scuppers drained it out of the cockpit slowly while I ran off toward the shore.

The fishing boat stopped where I'd been putzing around looking for Roger. They could have seen him go over, if they'd been looking with a glass. I hoped they'd find him. At that water temperature, you have about one to two hours to live before you lose enough body heat to finish you. A strong swimmer might find his way to shore, but the closer to shore you came, the worse the currents.

I ran off from them, looking back from time to time to try to see what they were doing. I couldn't spare the attention to really watch them, but I didn't think they'd picked him up. A powerboat came up behind them, went past, and veered out in a direct line with Port Angeles. It was much bigger than the boat that passed me in the Inlet, and I didn't see anything else on the water. It looked like I was all alone.

I tried to signal the powerboat. I flashed a light at it, waved my arms, and finally when nothing happened I lit off a red flare. It went right on by, a mile away, and I supposed the skipper was too intent on getting through that slop to look around toward the shore. The flare just showed the fishing boat where I was, so I threw it overboard.

I was rushing down toward the shore now, and although there was still enough light for me to tell where I was, that wouldn't last very long. If I hit rock at that speed it would tear the bottom right out of *Witch*. For that matter, mud wouldn't be much better with the seas we had. The waves would lift *Witch* up and drop her again, and no sailboat or any other kind of boat can take that kind of pounding for long. There's no beach either, except at Dungeness Spit, and that was off to windward. With the surf these waves would throw at the cliff edges in front of me, the boat had to survive for me to live through the night. Two hours in the water would finish me as fast as it was going to finish Roger.

I was mad clear through. I was mad at Roger, the weather, the fishing boat, Shearing, and for that matter, myself. I was even a little sorry for Roger. I had delayed that jibe stunt just a little too long, hoping to get identification of the boat that would meet him. Well, I'd got it all right. The problem was, what could I do with it?

As for Roger, I could have got him overboard any time after we rounded Point Wilson. There would have been enough time and daylight to fish him out again, and afterwards I could have run in under the shelter of Protection Island and anchored. Now I was in trouble.

The fishing boat was bearing down on me, and even without it there wasn't much sea room. To shorten sail, I would have to heave to and reef. But a boat hove to makes leeway, at least a couple of knots, and I was less than a mile from a lee shore. There was some question as to whether I could get the boat to safety even without Roger's friends behind me. I should be able to run along the shore to Port Angeles, although it's not very safe from an easterly or northeasterly storm, but I wouldn't know until I reached there. It didn't matter anyway. Long before I could reach shelter, the fishing boat would catch up with me.

I didn't look for much help from Shearing's crew. The wind was coming up stronger and stronger, and every other wave was a breaker. Unless they had an experienced sailor aboard, this was no weather for a pleasure-type power cruiser, with its big cabin and high windage areas. The fishing boat, of course, wasn't in any difficulty at all. She'd be rolling heavily now, shaking everybody and everything up, but those boats are designed with Alaska storms in mind, not just the stuff Juan de Fuca can throw at you. Not that old Juan is anybody to have mad at you, you understand. He's got tricks with big tide-augmented seas that even the Pacific Coast can't match. We lose a pleasure boat or two out here every year, when some hardy soul refuses to run for shelter, or gets caught where there isn't any.

Witch was built to take this sort of thing a lot better than a powerboat, but her designers never intended her to carry this much sail in winds gusting to forty or forty-five knots. I had to get some more sail down or something would carry away.

Looking behind me, I saw that the fishing boat was still circling around, so that there was a mile or so between us now. It would take some time for them to close the gap, since I didn't think they could get more than three knots difference between our speeds. If I stood still it would take them six or eight minutes to catch me.

There looked like one chance. Ahead of me about two miles was the pier I had built. In those seas and without a motor, I couldn't put into the dock and tie up, but given a little time I did have a chance of getting ashore. I ran on toward the pier, getting a compass bearing on where I could find it in case it was too dark to see when I reached there. I wasn't sure I wanted a light, because the fishing boat could see me, but in the dark it's hard to sail. It didn't look like I could win either way.

When I reached the dock, the fishing boat had swung around so that I could see both the red and green bow lights. She was headed directly for me. Two hundred feet from shore, I swung *Witch* around into the wind, feeling her heel until her rail was under, and tacked, once again, leaving the jib to windward. She was hove to, drifting off to leeward but holding her own for a moment. I opened the forehatch, grabbed my big anchor, and threw it and its chain over. I just prayed I'd judged this whole thing right.

Now that I was committed, the next thing was to get the sails down. I left them in a shapeless bundle, the jib tied with its own sheet to the stay, and the main bundled in a crazy pile around the boom. I wound line around it to hold it down, and then went forward again.

I had cut it close, but I was upwind of the dock. By paying out anchor line I was able to move *Witch* closer and closer to the pier, using the tiller to swing her from side to side as I needed to. It really didn't take long to get her the hundred feet or so to the dock, but it seemed like hours. The water is shallow near the shore, six fathoms, so the waves were building up high, but it was possible to reach the dock from the boat if you jumped just right. I cleated a line to the stern of the boat, held the end, and dived onto the float. My legs went in the water, but I managed to scramble on, all the wind knocked out of me for the moment. There wasn't another boat at the dock; my client was away.

When I stood up the fishing boat was bearing down on me. With their big engines they could maneuver close to the dock, and I didn't want to be there when they came. I ran along the pier to the shore, reaching it just as the fish boat came along the lee side. The first thing I saw was a man with a rifle.

He didn't say a word, just took aim and fired. With

the boat rolling like that he didn't have much chance of hitting me, but there wasn't any place for me to go. They'd soon get off the boat and finish me. I looked up the stairway to the top, but I didn't think I had a chance of getting there. It would be like giving them target practice.

Elmer, my client, had a little storehouse hollowed out of the bank next to where his stairway went up. I saw it, thought about it for a second, and grabbed a rock, pounding away on the padlock. While I was doing this the rifleman kept up a steady fire, and his partner brought the boat up to the dock. It didn't look like there were more than two aboard.

I got the locker open about the time one of them got off the boat and tied up. He waited for his partner, and I figured they didn't know I was unarmed. I scrambled into the little cave, hoping that I wasn't wrong about what I'd find there.

I wasn't. An open dynamite box, with five sticks left in it, was off to one side, and on a shelf was a little Styrofoam box of detonating caps with fuse. I got my knife out and cut a random length of fuse, shoved it in a cap, and crimped the mess with my teeth. The marline-spike on my pocketknife made a good hole in a stick of dynamite, and I shoved the cap in it. Then I lit the end of another piece of fuse.

Outside, one of them was still aboard the fishing boat, and as I looked out he played a spotlight directly on the open door of the little dirt storehouse. The rifle-man was standing on the dock next to the boat, and made gestures with his free hand to indicate I should come out. They were about forty feet away.

The fuse hissed away while I got another cap crimped and shoved into a stick. It doesn't really take long, and although I hadn't had any CIA courses, there are few civil engineers who aren't familiar with *The Blaster's Handbook*. The stuff isn't any more dangerous than any other tool if you know what you're doing.

When I had two sticks, I lit the fuse of the second by holding my burning fuse against it, giving myself about ten seconds worth of burn time. Then I stepped to the

edge of the storehouse and threw it toward the fishing
boat, jumping back inside before the rifleman could get
a shot at me.

The wind and my shelter muffled the sound of the
stuff going off. When I heard it, I ran out, holding my
other stick and the lit fuse. The rifleman wasn't standing there anymore, but somebody was attending the
spotlight. It figured that the stick had landed somewhere near the gunman, and knocked him off into the
water.

I used the burning end of the fuse to light the other
stick down close to the cap, ran forward, and pitched
the stick up on the deck of the fishing boat, right behind
the wheel house. Then I lay flat on the dock and waited.

Unless it's packed in, a single stick of dynamite won't
do all that much damage, but it's still a lot of power. It
tore the wheelhouse roof off, and I didn't think
anybody in there was going to be interested in shooting
me. As I got up, the boat drifted away from me.

They had cleated the boat by taking an end of the
mooring lines around the cleats on the dock, then bringing them back aboard and making them fast amidships.
This is a convenient technique and pretty standard
because it lets you cast yourself loose without any help
and without having to jump for the boat after she's
loose. My second stick of dynamite had either torn the
cleat loose, or cut the lines, because she was drifting
away fast now. There wasn't a thing I could do about it.
She'd either end up in Port Angeles or on the rocks
along the coast before you get there. I didn't see how
she could get to Port Angeles.

As for myself, I wasn't sure I wanted to be on that
pier in the morning. Furthermore, I didn't want to
abandon *Witch*. She was riding all right out there, her
stern about four feet from the dock, but if that anchor
dragged just a little bit she'd pound to pieces on the
float. I took the stern line I'd made fast on the windward side—the fishing boat had naturally come up on
the lee side of the dock, as I would have if I'd had any
fuel for the motor—and used it to pull myself back
aboard *Witch*. Then I took in enough line to get her

back out away from there, and started to tidy her up. The wind wasn't getting any stronger, and a lot of times in the Straits you'll have something like a gale in the evening, only to have dead calm the next morning. I didn't think this would last. Just in case, I pulled *Witch* out even farther, let the second anchor over the side, and payed out scope so that both were holding. Then I went below, changed to some dry clothes, laid out my oilskins in case I'd need them, and went to sleep. It was probably a tom-fool thing to do, but after fighting that tiller all day, I would have been ready to pass out even if I hadn't been up all night before.

12

I WOKE UP at four thirty because somebody was calling my name with a bullhorn. As I shook the sleep out of my head, it seemed the seas were a lot calmer, and I didn't hear the angry scream of the wind tearing at the rigging. It was chilly in the cabin after being under the blankets, and I pulled my yellow windproof jacket on before going out on deck.

Somebody had a spotlight in my eyes. The bullhorn said, "Paul, are you all right?" It was a man's voice, and I didn't recognize it. Then a girl shouted from the dark, "Paul?" The wind was still around fifteen to twenty knots, and she didn't have the bullhorn, but it was Janie all right. They were upwind of me, which was stupid, and I decided nobody aboard their boat really knew what he was doing. If their motors quit they'd drift right down on me.

I motioned them to come around to the lee side, and as they moved they got the blasted spot out of my eyes. It was the power cruiser I'd seen in the Inlet. I made enough hand signals and shouts to finally get over to them the idea that they'd have to throw me a line if they wanted me aboard, and when they did I got it around my waist and let them pull me. I went in to my knees for the second time that night before I scrambled up the side to their deck.

George was at the wheel, with Janie standing next to him. Down below in the cabin, Doug was trying to keep his guts from coming up, having long since lost everything he had eaten in the last couple of days. A gravelly voiced middle-aged guy with a potbelly did the hauling to get me aboard.

"Where's Balsinger?" George asked me as soon as I

was aboard. I pointed over the side. While he was pondering that, Janie came over to me, put her hands on my shoulders, and looked at me for what seemed like a long time. Then she sat down on the stool opposite the helmsman's seat.

"What kept you?" I asked George.

"That damn storm," he shouted. It really wasn't all that loud on board, but I supposed he had got in the habit of shouting when the wind was stronger. "We got in the bay there behind the spit, and the waves were so damn big I thought we'd sink. I had to run in under Protection Island to get out of the storm. Been looking for you for two hours."

"Thanks a whole bunch, buddies," I said. I really wasn't mad at them. With that big windcatcher cabin and the huge transom there was a real chance the boat would be swamped if you didn't know how to handle her, and George obviously didn't.

"Janie wanted us to come after you," he said. Potbelly added, "Wanted us to? The chick damn near mutinied."

I looked over at her. "I'm glad somebody worried about me."

"We didn't know what we could do anyway, Paul," she said. "George thought Balsinger would shoot you if we got close to you and he kept saying you were a sailor and Balsinger wasn't, so I shouldn't worry. I guess he was right."

"Hell, Balsinger wasn't any trouble," I told them. "Him I could handle, it was his two friends in the fishing boat that almost got me."

Janie jumped up. "You see, I knew we ought to follow Paul," she told George. He wasn't very interested in what she said, but he turned to me and asked, "Where is this fishing boat? Can you identify it?"

"Sure," I told him. "Easy as pie. It's the fishing boat with the cabin top blown apart by a stick of dynamite. I'd look off the rocks just before you get to Port Angeles, if you really want to find it. There'll probably be pieces all along the shore from there to Ediz Hook and beyond."

"What in hell did you do?" he demanded.

Potbelly went into the cabin and started fussing with the radio while I explained what had happened to everybody. When I got to the part about dynamiting the fishing boat, George looked unhappy, but he didn't say anything.

Potbelly called out, "Radio for you. Now." I went below, and he told it, "Here's Larry. Over."

There wasn't any question as to who was talking. With some people electronics makes quite a change in their voices, but Shearing sounded like he was coming over a radio all the time, if you know what I mean.

"I take it your friend is enjoying a trip in somewhat warmer climate. Over," the box said. Potbelly told me this wasn't a secure circuit, whatever that meant, and handed me the mike.

"Yeah, and his friends too. Over."

"It is important that the Neighbors don't find out we saw him off. They might have the wrong idea. Can you do something? Over."

"We could come home. Will that do? Over."

"It will have to if that's all you think of. Do so. Out."

I told George, and then came the perfect bitch of a job of getting back aboard *Witch* in that wind. I took a line with me, and after I got the anchor up they towed me off toward Admiralty Inlet. They towed her too fast, but nothing came apart, so we were back in Seattle by early afternoon. This job was costing me all my sleep.

We had the meeting in Shearing's office downtown. You reach it by going to an insurance brokerage office, from which, if you know how, you can reach an adjoining suite.

I told him the whole story, about the chase and the cruise, and the sinking of the fishing boat. He didn't say a word while I told it, just made little marks on the paper in front of him. This time he was drawing sailboats, little ones, big ones, and boats with an absolutely insane rigging scheme. After I finished, I asked him, "Why did that fishing boat attack me on sight like that? It still doesn't make that much sense."

"It makes very good sense. Your guess as to what they would do with Roger if they found him was probably a good one. Since they had orders to kill him, and they couldn't be sure who had gone overboard, they went right ahead with the job. They would want to finish you both and sink your boat while the storm kept any traffic out of the Straits. Is there any chance the Coast Guard can tell there was an explosion aboard the fishing boat?"

"If there's enough fishing boat left to examine after the rocks get through with it, yes," I told him. "But I doubt that they'll know it was dynamite. Lots of things explode on boats, particularly gasoline." I lit my pipe, thought for a second of the conditions along that stretch of coast, and said, "Unless they go in for salvage operations, they won't find it if they haven't already."

"Then I think we can forget about the fishing boat. What of Balsinger? Will he be found?"

"How should I know? I had him put on a life jacket, he should float, so I'd say there was a reasonable chance he'll wash up somewhere and be found. But lots of people who go overboard in the Straits never are."

He thought about that for a minute. "In case they do, I'll release enough evidence on him so that the police will be looking for him on a narcotics charge. They can devise their own theories of how he got there. We have his book deciphered, and that will clean up most of the narcotics organization. It also helps a little in understanding the espionage group, but not much. Pity you couldn't bring him in alive . . ." He drew a battleship firing into the little flotilla of sailboats, lit a Camel, and looked at me again. "We didn't get the top men, you know. But we have cut off their sources of money for a while, which will slow down their espionage activities. We even recovered quite a bit of their money, which will come in handy for things like your boat."

"I really am sorry I didn't get him alive," I said. I meant it, too. When he first said that, I had started to say something sarcastic, then I realized that Shearing knew as well as I did what he had said and how he meant it.

"Yes. Well, the narcotics organization is rather thoroughly destroyed. Louis took in most of the pushers and distributors. We have also given him Richard Wahlke, and there's sufficient evidence even with today's courts to send him to prison for a while. The girl, Nancy Snow, claims she thought the bags they took out of the film boxes contained LSD and were being distributed to a secret religious organization. We are inclined to believe her, and I think she will get off with probation. She met the Wahlke boy through Carole Halleck, by the way. We still don't see just where the Halleck girl fit in.—Oh, and Nancy Snow also says she knows for a fact that you were not aware of the contents of those film boxes. The Halleck girl told her. So you won't be charged with anything." He stopped talking, finished his cigarette, and looked at his drawing. Then he looked back at me. "You see what this adds up to?"

I didn't, and told him so.

"None of that group who knew you to be involved with us are alive. If any of them who ever heard of you are left, and that's doubtful, they know of you only as an unwitting courier. Your cover is still in good shape, except for getting out a story of your break with the Halleck girl before she was killed. So if you want a job looking for the rest of that group, it's still open. For an untrained man, you didn't do too badly at all."

I thought about this for a minute. I wanted to tell him to shove it, with his offer of a career in the junior spy business. He sucked me into this thing, and now I was damn well out of it. But I thought about drainage systems and that racket, and I wasn't very interested in them. I could see myself sitting in my house, staring at plans for structures I didn't care about, thinking about Janie and George and seasick Doug, and it didn't make a good picture. There was something about the last couple of weeks. I had never felt more alive in my life, and now it was over, and I didn't really want it to be. Finally, I didn't say anything. I just looked at him.

"You've got time," he told me. "Actually you've got a training class coming. It starts in five days, runs two weeks. You should have had it before we put you on this mission, so you can take it now and still quit when it's over. We owe you that."

"I'll let you know," I told him.

"You do that. Through Janie. I want you to help her ease out of the relationship with you as the rest of the District sees it. And you ought to get it out that you and Carole Halleck had a fight and she left mad. Janie's expecting you at seven tonight at her apartment. You don't mind, do you?"

It hurt when he mentioned Carole, but it wouldn't do her any good, and to be honest I couldn't tell if it was just that she kept me from being alone. I remembered Janie, and how she'd been worried about me and how at least I wouldn't sit tonight in that room, feeling someone behind me was reading a book and looking at me over the top of it. I walked to the door, stopped, and looked back at him. "No, I don't mind," I told him.